AF493007

I dedicate this to the women who were told while growing up, that they were underserving of greatness. To them I say, you can be far greater than you have ever believed yourself to be.

Tamara Zantout is the author of Drawing Lines, a book that explores identity through street art. She is the founder of the Urban Fusion, a publishing house for Art books and that caters for self-publishing authors. She is an editor, designer, art director and sound producer. Her passion as a pilot, has often led her to explore hidden islands. Culturally as well as geographically, Zantout has lived between the East and West, having spent most of her childhood in London, during the war in Lebanon. She has worked in various fields some in Economic journalism and the UNDP and others in the fields of design and production, as well as Saatchi in advertising, with multiple degrees both at the undergraduate and graduate level, from Architecture at the Architectural Association in London, to Economics and a master's degree in Urban Planning. She has acted as copywriter for several novels and large projects. In her many writings, she has often sought to bridge the gap between the two worlds.

Contents

The Sunsets Of Avalon

Tamara Zantout
The Sunsets Of Avalon I

First edition, June 2023

Published by The Urban Fushion
info@theurbanfusion.com

Printed and bound in Great Britain by IngramSpark

ISBN 9789693092240

Cover Illustration: Adra Kandil
Book design: Ghada Noueiry

Also by Tamara Zantout
Drawing Lines, 2018

The Sunsets of Avalon

Part 1

A Play by Tamara Zantout

THE PERSONS OF THE PLAY

NYMANNE   the Lady of the Lake

LORD PENDRAGON   her father

GAWAIN   her son; later Knight of the Round Table

KAY   her son; later Knight of the Round Table

MERLIN   powerful sorcerer

ARTHUR   half brother to Nymanne; later King of Camelot

MORDRED   father to Gawain and Kay

MAEVE   general to the Amazons

ROISÌN   Amazon warrior

IGRAINE   mother to Nymanne

EVÀ   sister to Nymanne

MADOC   brother to Nymanne

EDMUND   brother to Nymanne

MORRÌGAN   wife to Edmund

KING CONCHOBAR   nefarious leader

THE GESTER OF BORDOVA   advisor to the king

ENAREES   Scythian priest and warlord

KISSAR   servant of Enarees

ACT I
The Nexus

Scene 1

Scene 1 opens on the shore between Camlann and Avalon at dawn. The first rays of sunlight pierce through the mist and filter through the trees, creating a whimsical dance of light.

Behind a seemingly peaceful morning, echoes of conflict ripple in the distance. As we wearily approach the war zone, as impartial witnesses, a very stark picture is revealed. Hordes of power-hungry men are violently seeking to oppress an army of women, who are backed by a handful of knights, valiantly supporting their cause. And has this not been the plight of women since the dawn of time, dear reader? These daily battles have very oft been hiding in plain sight.

A powerful wizard and sorceress stand side by side seeking to dispel the king's army of mercenaries. Merlin and Nymanne fend off the attacks of King Conchobar's army and Enarees's Militia with magic disarming spells, protecting the women and children on the barges behind them.

Young Arthur and his knights battle to ward off the attacks on the front lines with the Amazon warriors by their side.

MERLIN
They're preparing to catapult the fire stones! Everyone retreat behind me! Arthur! Fall back!

Arthur and the Amazons swiftly retreat to board the barges and reach Merlin's side.

MERLIN

Nymanne! I need you to ward off the projectiles until I can conjure the shield!

Nymanne panicked and trying to muster her strength, aims for a catapult as it is being armed in the distance, anticipating the strike. It breaks in mid formation and rotates wildly, landing on a broken trunk with one end suspended in mid air, while the other end, carrying the projectile, rests on the ground with the fire still ablaze.

Merlin begins to chant the sacred words of the old religion to raise a powerful shield. Meanwhile, Gawain, a young lad of twelve, who has spotted the flaming catapult, makes a dash towards it, breaking away from the group. He manages to stealthily jump past them to the shore, just as Merlin raises his shield. Nymanne looks to her son panic stricken.

NYMANNE

Gawain! Gawain come back! Stop! What are you doing?

Gawain pays no heed to his mother's cries and continues determinedly on his dash towards the catapult. Nymanne turns to Merlin imploringly.

NYMANNE

Merlin! Open the shield! Open it now! Gawain is out there!

MERLIN

I will expose everyone to the catapults. I can't break the shield are you mad?

Nymanne turns towards Merlin, threatening to use her magic.

NYMANNE

Please don't make me use my magic against you. I'm not leaving my son out there.

MERLIN

Nymanne. I beg you, think about what you're doing.

NYMANNE

I will kill you if I must. Open the shield now!

Gawain oblivious to the tension he has instigated, makes a dash towards the catapult, while fire balls continue to fall all around him. Nymanne and Merlin continue to face off in tense confrontation.

Scene 2

In a forest in Cornwall, on the borders of Avalon, two characters are shielded within a tree enclosure. Behind them lies a village torn apart by ravages of conflict. It is a desolate sight, filled with bloodshed and ruins of a once lush and prosperous village.

Mordred is not of tall stature. His small eyes are dark and piercing, with a hint of cruelty that is ever present. The scar across his eyebrow further accentuates the darkness of his stare. His black hair is tied and pulled at the back.

MORDRED

"I shall not finance your sunsets", he says dismissively, with a hint of disdain, "if it is Avalon you seek, then you shall seek it alone, without the children."

Nymanne stands in disbelief, carefully weighing her words. It took every ounce of her being to contain her rage towards this man, one whom she could no longer fathom, was the father of her children. Her long brown hair braided at the top of her head, falls in long waves at her waist. Though it was not the custom, she wore leather trousers, to avoid the unwarranted glare of men, as she had ventured recklessly across many lands, in order to reach the border. She carried her children with her, alone into the dark of night. She had ventured across many battlefields, risked everything, and now... "What protected you, and what continues to protect you", she thinks, "is that they love you, nothing more". Her iris sharpens as she glares at him, like a lioness ready to pounce.

She is the daughter of Lord Pendragon, and he the leader of mercenaries, men for hire that kill on command. That is after all, what he did best. Her brother had been against this marriage. How she wished she had headed his warnings. But she had received a vision. An answer to her long unanswerable question: "From the fires of hell shall you receive two angels, higher souls that are destined for greatness. You are their true guardian. You alone shall be entrusted with raising them, to uphold the highest orders of valour and courage in the face of adversity. And adversity there shall be. They must battle those they love the most, in the face of evil, to fight for what is right and restore the balance of nature." The Great Mother Modron had visited her in a dream. She foretold what must be. What was always meant to be. "So it is written", said the voice in her mind.

NYMANNE

You speak as though this is the promised land, Mordred. This is a city on the brink of war. The recent attack destroyed an entire village and killed hundreds. They have used a magic powder that spread like a mushroom across the skies, wiping out all in its wake. And now, there are seldom any resources left to survive on, food, water, sustenance is scarce. Is this truly the environment you wish for them?

He holds his gaze, the iris becoming almost indiscernible. His face looking strangely empty of expression. She knew it was impossible to reach him. She wondered if he was ever human at all.

MORDRED

If you can't handle a few explosions, then perhaps you should have the children live with me.

NYMANNE

I have negotiated safe passage into the border, I have secured shelter for them by lake Llyn Ogwen, the lake of the mystics. They will be safe there, living in peace, until they can grow into the men they are meant to become. All you need do now, is instruct your men to step aside. You will see them Mordred, I will negotiate safe passage for you as well.

MORDRED

It is not the role of women to decide on the future of men. You would do well to remember your place.

NYMANNE

I know my place! It is as warrior and protector of these young souls, it is my mission, and I will not allow you to hide behind worldly transgressions of the laws of nature, in this desolate land, that has lost all sense of reason and integrity. Perhaps it is time you remember with whom you speak, Mordred.

MORDRED

He sniggers, half smiling. "I know to whom I speak." He looks around him. "Your fathers' men are not with you; does he know you are here?"

She was so weary of having to answer to men, when all reason had gone from them. But this was Camlann, a land governed by men, senseless, greedy men of war. They had forgotten the ways of the old religion, when powerful matriarchies governed these lands, when peace was the constant state of rule. The lands of Avalon were still true to the goddess Mother, they honored the power of the Divine Feminine, that binds Earth and Heaven together.

NYMANNE

"I urge you one last time, tell your men to stand down and allow us safe passage. All you need do is step aside; I will take care of the rest. Think of their future, Mordred, their welfare, their safety." She implored.

MORDRED

There is no future in Avalon.

NYMANNE

"And there is one here amongst the destruction and desolation?", she yells in disbelief, gesturing towards the misery around her.

MORDRED

"My men will ensure you return to your fathers dominion safely." He responds unfazed, with a hardened look, almost of sadistic pleasure.

NYMANNE

Her eyes flash in anger. "They will ensure our safe return, or that we do not find an alternative means of reaching Avalon?" She questions defiantly.

MORDRED

"By whichever way you choose to look at it, you shall not enter Avalon and perform your witchery. I shall not finance your sunsets." He asserts, rather pleased with himself.

NYMANNE

"You will regret this" she says as she walks away, suppressing her anger.

Scene 3

LORD PENDRAGON

You specifically disobeyed me! I told you not to go against him, but you went nonetheless and alone! How could you risk the children's lives in this way?

Lord Pendragon was not a forgiving man, he punished anyone who disobeyed him. But this daughter of his, was the only one who challenged him of all of his children.

NYMANNE

"You said you would stand by me". She responds almost accusingly, measuring her words. "I asked you, if I went despite him, despite his madness, to save these children from their father's selfish pride, would you stand with me."

LORD PENDRAGON

"I regret having said that." He looks down. "I gave it a second thought and felt it unwise."

NYMANNE

"Before challenging him, I asked you if I had your support. You promised me it would be unwavering, till the end." She whispers, choking on her words.

"I know what I said." He replies loudly, slamming his fist on the armrest of his elevated throne.

NYMANNE

"I did what I had to do, to save them. If no one else was to stand by me, then so be it." She raises her head defiantly.

LORD PENDRAGON

You cannot proceed against my wishes!

NYMANNE

Father, you have taught me in the powers of the mind, in the art of battle. I have trained with the greatest swordsmen, I have travelled far and wide, I have learnt all that there is to learn, I have read endless libraries of books, I have mastered what most men have not, and yet you tell me that I need permission to decide on the welfare of my own children? On how best to protect them from their father's ignorance? It does not take much to know that

Camlann is falling. Why would you wish them to stay in this land of misery?

LORD PENDRAGON
It will get better my child. They are electing a new senate.
NYMANNE
The senate of the same half puppet men ruled by that sleeping King Conchobar? We are being governed by the undead! Lord knows if they have struck a bargain with the devil himself. No disease befalls them, yet they are so old they often fall motionless to the floor! Perhaps his Jester is his puppet master, that little fool that always walks beside him.

LORD PENDRAGON
My child you must watch yourself. A woman is not to speak of politics in these lands.

NYMANNE
Because I am half a man father? Isn't that what you have told me, time and time again? Isn't that what your religion has said?

LORD PENDRAGON
It is your religion as well.

NYMANNE
If I was born into it, it does not mean that I have embraced it.

LORD PENDRAGON
You misunderstand, a woman is not to vote or voice her political opinion because the religion understands that she would be influenced to speak her husband's mind and not her own.

NYMANNE

How can you say such things? As though women are puppets who can be manipulated into subjugation! How can you say this when it is in fact your very own son that is being manipulated by his spouse?

LORD PENDRAGON

"We do not know this for sure." He looks down, swallowing with difficulty.

NYMANNE

Do we not? Is he acting of sound mind?

LORD PENDRAGON

"No." He utters, barely mouthing his reply.

NYMANNE

And yet you gave him dominion over most of your lands while he continues to act foolishly, wasting the crops and causing the farmers to starve! And I, what role have you assigned me?

LORD PENDRAGON

Why must we continue to speak of this? The religion states that a woman shall have dominion over half that of her brothers, that is the law. Thus it is written and so it shall be.

NYMANNE

Those days are over!

LORD PENDRAGON

My child, again I believe the religion to be true in its logic. Women receive half that of men because they are wed into their husband's dominion.

NYMANNE

I am not married. It was a glorious day when I freed myself of such unholy bonds. Thus your statement holds no weight, father.

LORD PENDRAGON

"Do not speak over me! I have explained the wisdom of our God. Our most sacred God and his prophet." He begins reciting the sacred verses, almost automatically, in a means to silence her.

NYMANNE

"*Haec forma et omnia quae noto plicentur*" her voice vibrates through space; she whispers so he cannot hear. The soldiers behind Pendragon are frozen and stand motionless, Pendragon's lips halt in suspension, a bird in flight in the windowsill floats in mid-flight.

She stands in the silent hallway, all those in the chamber are still, suspended in time. She sighs in relief. Savouring this moment, standing taller than she had before. A white female shadow appears before her.

MODRON

"My child, what you conjure, you must repay." The shadow whispers softly. "Why have you senselessly wasted this gift?"

NYMANNE

Forgive me Great Mother, I could no longer be told that I was less than.

MODRON

"You know very well that you are not." The whisper echoes softly, an energy ripples through her as a blessing.

NYMANNE

When confronted with so much negativity from the very person I value most. It is as if a blade were piercing my heart. All that I have sought to become, was in part to make him proud.

MODRON

And so he is, though he knows not how to express it.

NYMANNE

"I find that difficult to fathom. Thank you, Great Mother, my power is depleting, I cannot hold time much longer." Her arms begin to tremble.

MODRON

The shadow whispers in an echo before it disappears: "Have faith Nymanne, all that must be, shall be. You shall find your true place, in this life and in the next."

Scene 4

These were indeed troubled times, the passage of the Kings men rampaging through the fields, were endangering the crops. They roamed the villages looking to pillage and plunder, while the King's merciless laws had already starved the people. There was no end to his lascivious greed, while his days were numbered, he continued on his aimless slumber in the safe confines of his castle, constantly wanting more recompense for his lack of governance. According to Celtic tradition, a true worthy king, had to be of good origin and standing, he had to be physically fit, and comply with the initiation ritual. This king was none of those things.

He had stumbled upon the throne by forging a secret alliance with the Scythian forces. He slumbered while they governed the lands, pillaging and looting much in their wake, transgressing all the laws of nature.

MADOC

"We shall continue to do what we can" says Madoc, surveying the fields. "I have engineered this new crop; it will survive the winter's cold. Instruct the villagers to plant these seeds on the parcels of barren land." He commands his workers, gesturing towards the endless fields to the west.

Madoc stands tall. He wears his lordly attire with pride, with the Pendragon seal at his chest. Yet he felt burdened by the weight of his new responsibilities. He did not expect to assume his brothers' tasks in addition to his own. "Edmund, what is this curse that has befallen you?" He thinks to himself, with great sadness. He surveys the fields and ponders on what he can do to make things better, for everyone. Perhaps he can bring about peace once more to the family. He had attempted to reason with his brother so many times before. But it was to no avail, it was like conversing with an empty shell, he could no longer reach him. Every other member of the family had given up on him. Nymanne had warned him to no longer make attempts to reason with him, that he was lost forever, trapped. He refused to believe it.

The winds howl around him, signalling the coming of the winter, and a foreboding of difficult times ahead. "There must be a way to make it all right." He thinks.

He sees the men returning in haste, almost frightened.

MAN 1

"My Lord, there is an insurgence. The people are refusing to sow the seeds, they say it is witchery. They are marching here as we speak." A worker claims, panic stricken.

MADOC

"You must go and seek reinforcements at once! Gather our army, and inform Lord Pendragon, I will hold them off for as long as I can. Go! Men follow me." He brandishes his sword.
"No one attacks unless I give the order. Hold steady. We have no desire for bloodshed."

The villagers walk en masse. They look angered and prepared for a rebellion against their lord. Madoc walks ahead of his men signalling a call for dialogue instead of combat.

A designated leader amongst the villagers walks ahead as well.

VILLAGER 1

My Lord, you have given us false seeds, our crops have all but dried out, we shall no longer follow your instructions; while our people continue to starve.

MADOC

"To what do I owe this strange superstition?" He asks bewildered, "We gain nothing from spoiling your crops."

VILLAGER 2

"Your power has waned over your lands; we will no longer yield to you!" said someone in the back of the crowd.

The angry villagers charge towards the soldiers. The village leader on the front lines makes desperate attempts to assuage the crowd.

Madoc bewildered seems unwilling to cause bloodshed.

MADOC
"Hold!" he yells out to his men brandishing his fist in the air, undecided as to what he must do next.

SWORDSMAN
"My Lord, they are not armed but they are too many." Mumbles one of his men, staring at the crowd advancing towards them.

Masked female warriors appear as though out of nowhere. They charge first against the villagers attempting to contain them. Madoc's men proceed to help. Madoc, exasperated, follows suit.

MADOC
"Disarm and contain only!" He yells, resigned.

The bronze women appear as Amazons, wearing leather trousers and wrapped pleated leather tops. They throw ropes and proceed to contain the crowd.

MADOC
"Who are you?" asks Madoc, "and why do you help us?"
One woman steps out.

LEADER OF THE AMAZONS
We seek to avoid needless bloodshed my Lord. You can thus set an example against the insurgence, without instigating further

violence.

MADOC

I do not wish for bloodshed either.

LEADER OF THE AMAZONS

I would advise you to imprison those responsible until order is restored, but no more. I hope you shall heed my advice.

She gestures to her amazons to withdraw.

MADOC

"I will indeed." He says, looking back at the forest from whence the women had disappeared.

Deep in the forest the women gather in their hideout. One of the amazons turns to her leader.

MAEVE

My lady, why did you not reveal your identity to your brother?

Nymanne removes her mask.

NYMANNE

"For him to know my identity is of no consequence. It will be difficult to fight our battles, if my father should be informed of my involvement. Let us continue to help bring peace at a distance. That is all we can do for now."

MAEVE

But to remain forever hidden as such? Veiling our true power, lying to our men? How long must we maintain this dumbfoolery?

NYMANNE

"For as long as it takes Maeve." Nymanne places her hand on her shoulder reassuringly. "As long as we remain hidden, we can still act freely. This world has been distorted to fear the power of the feminine. Any woman with power is branded a witch and burned at the stake. It is the easy way to subjugate half of a population and convince women that they must remain weak, if they are to be part of this world."

MAEVE

"It is an ill world." Replies Maeve in disdain.

NYMANNE

Indeed, it is. But the more women we can awaken from their induced slumber, the more we can succeed in achieving a harmonious world. One of equality. Be patient my dear friend. It shall come. I must return to the palace before they can notice my absence. Hold the fort until my return.

Nymanne makes her way out of the forest, stealthily infiltrating between the trees.

Scene 5

LORD PENDRAGON

"This is treason!" yells Lord Pendragon enraged, slamming his fist on the mantle of his throne. "Why would the villagers rise up against us? They have no reason to." He turns, as Nymanne enters the great hall. "Where have you been all morning Nymanne?"

NYMANNE

"Apologies father, I was called upon to visit the southern lands, the women wanted to consult me regarding the solstice festival."

LORD PENDRAGON

"So early in the season? Oh well, be that as it may, you should not wander too far my child, there is an insurgence amongst the villagers."

NYMANNE

"So I have heard father."

MADOC

"Father, they seem to believe in some sort of witchery, they have this strange notion that we are conspiring against them." Says Madoc, pondering the events of the day.

NYMANNE

"It is no conspiracy, there is a traitor in our midst." States Nymanne with intensity and deep thought.

LORD PENDRAGON

Whatever do you mean?

NYMANNE

There is a snake slithering its way amongst the people, whispering lies.

LORD PENDRAGON

"You mean?" ... He hesitates, in disbelief "Morrìgan?"

NYMANNE

"Yes."

LORD PENDRAGON

"It cannot be."

NYMANNE

"Why can it not be? Is there someone to silence her when she speaks ill of this family?" she questions accusingly.

LORD PENDRAGON

Nymanne please...

NYMANNE

Please stop excusing him father. He has brought shame to this family. All in the name of greed.

LORD PENDRAGON

"I beg you please." Whispers Pendragon, his face contorted with pain.

NYMANNE

"My apologies father for confronting you with a painful truth. But you must put an end to this. Lies can gain momentum, and if the wave is not contained in its course, it can grow to damaging heights." She asserts vehemently. "Evà, tell father what you have told me." She turns to her sister.

Evà saunters in, dressed as though she was to attend a ball. Her long blond hair flowing along her slender frame, her pale white skin making her appear almost fragile. She contrasted greatly with her sister, who had a more muscular frame and dark hair. Their eyes were also starkly different. Nymanne's green coloured eyes were highly attuned and sharp like that of a panther, while her sisters' small brown eyes complemented her very small, delicate face.

EVÀ

Well father, my very good friend princess Celesta of Gaulle, who was visiting her royal cousins, informed me at the ball we both attended only two evenings since, that she had to firmly contradict half-truths whispered by Morrìgan to her relatives. There were some very nasty lies father. Only I attempted to rise above them and not respond. Only I could not contradict her majesty when she very vehemently asked me to counter these lies to her cousins. We were distracted by the arrival of the singing barde, a very famous barde that had rode in from...

NYMANNE

"My dear sister, can we dispense with the pleasantries if you please, and focus on the subject at hand?" Nymanne wilfully interjects.

EVÀ

"How do you interrupt me so?" She huffs indignant, "I am your older sister after all."

NYMANNE

"Get to the point sister" Nymanne exhales, rolling her eyes.

EVÀ

"Father do you hear how she talks to me?" she exclaims

LORD PENDRAGON

"Get to the important part my child, please." He nods exhausted.

EVÀ

"Morrìgan is suggesting far and wide that we have lost dominion

over our lands, and that you..." she hesitates.
LORD PENDRAGON
That I what?

EVÀ
"That you..." She bites her lip hesitant, "that you are no longer of sound mind, and have no authority over your people."

Lord Pendragon attempts to preserve his countenance. He cannot veil his disbelief at the extend of his son's betrayal. "It cannot be" he thinks to himself.

LORD PENDRAGON
"Are you certain of this information?" he asks, his voice trembling.

NYMANNE
Don't you see father, if she spreads doubt amongst your people, then how can they respect and fear you? That is why they have risen against you. She has been sowing the seeds of doubt. Everywhere she ventures, she whispers her lies.

LORD PENDRAGON
What would she stand to gain from this? What does your brother do to stop her?

NYMANNE
If she weakens your hold upon your dominion, she hopes my brother can take your place.

LORD PENDRAGON
"He will not even wait for me to die first." He concludes painfully,

closing his eyes. "So that is why the lenders questioned my resolve when I wished to expand the cultivation of the lands."

NYMANNE

Yes. You must speak with him father. Order him to put an end to her deceit. This insurgence has been reigned in. But can we continue to forever cleanse the damage she causes to this family?

LORD PENDRAGON

"I will not." He states vehemently. "Words cannot harm me. Those who know me, know what I stand for, and who I am."

NYMANNE

Yes, but when your very own speak against you, what do you expect your people to believe?

LORD PENDRAGON

I will not entertain such baseless, petty actions.

NYMANNE

Father please, understand that these are very disparaging actions, that can have devastating effects. Words are not mere words.

LORD PENDRAGON

I will not.

NYMANNE

Sister will you speak with him?

EVÀ

"When we spoke last, I mentioned she had been spreading false rumours about this family, about my very husband. He only replied on the offensive, calling me a liar. He defends her blindly, denying any wrongdoing on her part. He is perfectly at peace with the damage her actions are inflicting. He will not rise against her.

NYMANNE

What is this blind allegiance he carries for her, when I have seen her disparage him with my own eyes, in front of even his children? She spoke with him in such an absurd manner, I could barely contain myself. He yields to her every whim, and yet rises against us?

LORD PENDRAGON

So, it seems.

Scene 6

MORRÌGAN

And are you suggesting I simply stand aside and watch, whilst you allow them to take everything?

EDMUND

Morrìgan, whatever do you mean? I am a Pendragon, and furthermore, I am the eldest! Everything would have fallen to me regardless of what you may or may not have done.

MORRÌGAN

It's time to remove them. They have to go.

EDMUND

But they are my family.
MORRÌGAN
"I am your only family now!" She replies firmly, then magically shifts her demeanour, continuing in a soft motherly tone. "Don't you recall our promise to each other, when we were married? We are the real family, the only one that matters. It is only me for you. My Mooha, my Moomooha. Moomoomoo", she says in a baby voice, whilst caressing his hair.

He yields to her. Always yields to her. Is it fear? Is it complacency? He did not know the reason.

EDMUND
What... what in the heavens are you doing Morrìgan?

MORRÌGAN
I am looking out for our best interests; I am only looking out for you.

EDMUND
"You are looking out for your best interests." He mumbles, almost to himself.

MORRÌGAN
"He is the problem. You must say it! Say it!" She screams, losing her countenance.

EDMUND
Morrìgan, I beg you leave me. Have you not done enough? When you set father and son against one another, there are consequences.

MORRÌGAN
"What I have done, I have done only for you!" She yells, her eyes

turning crimson. "I would not have needed to interfere, had you not acted like such a spineless little child!"

EDMUND

My entire family think the worst of me. They will no longer speak with me. My father seldom looks at me now.

MORRÌGAN

Do not place blame on me! I am simply managing what must be managed, removing what needs to be removed. I am only doing what you have been incapable of doing, because you are a flightless little bird!

EDMUND

"There is so much I can tolerate from you Morrìgan." He says looking to the ground.

She shifts her demeanour again, turning to him once more to caress his hair.

MORRÌGAN

"Remember that we are only stronger together. I am your family, my Moomoomoo..." she says, in a motherly tone.

Again, he yields.

ACT II
The Lake

Scene 1

VOICE

Awaken.

NYMANNE

The whispering voices of the night echo in the darkness, indiscernible to those who refuse to believe. Many have thus lost their souls and their innocence to the shadows. Many have lost the flame of childlike wonder.

VOICE

To the lake.

NYMANNE

I knew to which lake the voices had beckoned me, like overlaying whispers. In a single moment the clouds had overcast the sky and shrouded the sun. The moorlands surrounding it continue to whisper. They beckon me to walk to the lake. Many have feared this lake because they fail to grasp its magic. They say the lake is bottomless and links to the sea in an infinite abyss. The abyss is a source of endless power and mystery. It is not to be feared but must indeed be understood. Dozmary Pool, links both worlds together. The world of the spirits and that of the waking world. What most do not know, is that the otherworld is never separate from us. We are forever connected to it. It is believed to be a cursed lake, but many fear what they do not understand. How many of us who are different are looked upon as the cursed? Women who strive to prove their worth are branded as witches for their powers. It is the power of the mind and heart that guides us, gifted to us by the Great Mother. Some call her Mother Earth, others Modron, but whatever name she carries, what truly matters is preserving the balance of the universe.

THE VOICE

Enter.

NYMANNE

The earth and water call to me. I have too long been subdued by human interaction, far from the powers that be. My spirit must be cleansed. We often need respite from the lost world of men.

Nymanne enters the lake almost drawn to it by an enchanting force. Her long dark hair begins to simulate the movement of the lake as she reaches waist deep. Now fully transported, her long dress and cloak merge with the water, and begin to float in fluid motion. As she becomes more and more submerged, she experiences a sense of release, as though cleansed from all negative human interaction. The light of the full moon glistens, cradled by the water's movement. She is at home here. She senses an energy tingling at her fingertips and suddenly dives fully into the water. Beneath the depths, she notices a glowing form and swims towards it. She begins to dig out part of the glowing object buried beneath and notices a metallic sword. The sword remains firmly anchored and resists her as she tugs forcefully at it. Out of breath she resurfaces.

NYMANNE

"Not yet." She gasps, out of breath.

Nymanne exits the water feeling completely overwhelmed. What was the meaning of this strange apparition? Was this a sign of something she was destined for? She had no notion of what was to come, or what the powers wished of her. She looked to the moon for a message, a sign. But it remained silent, a witness to the magic beneath the surface of the water. Both radiated with a brilliant light, as though communicating with one another.

Scene 2

NYMANNE

What is it Maeve? I was summoned by your call of the sparrow-hawk and have come as swiftly as I could.

MAEVE

My lady, the grain silos are burning. They have mysteriously caught fire in the dead of night, while everyone sleeps. I have awakened the others. We are ready to do what is necessary.

NYMANNE

Where are the Kings guards? Have they not been sent to salvage the food stock of the Kingdom?

MAEVE

I waited an hour before calling you. No one is coming it seems.

NYMANNE

Then it must be the work of King Conchobar. He is hiding something. There is no chance the Kings guards were not yet alerted to the fire.

They watch the Silos burning in a raging fire, in the dead of night.

MAEVE

My Lady, we must stop this fire, the people will starve.

NYMANNE

I fear a trap. Why has no one yet come forth? We must slowly infiltrate the structure. Hide in the shadows, do not let anyone see you. Do not extinguish the fire. Salvage what you can of the grain and distribute them to the people. I will go investigate further. Roísín, you will accompany me. Bring your bow and arrows. I fear we will need them tonight.

The women separate in two teams. They walk stealthily in the shadows ensuring they aren't detected. Women of character in these parts of the world have grown accustomed to remaining invisible, in order to stay alive. It has become second nature to them, concealment is their strength.

The silos had already been pierced at the foundations. Large holes that threatened its imposing structure, much like the fire that continued to rage on. It was almost as though someone was adamant to erase all traces of these rising vertical landmarks. Maeve signals for everyone to stand before each gaping hole and retrieve the grain that flowed freely into their cloaks. Soon after, they disappear silently into the night.

Maeve worriedly takes one final glance backwards for Nymanne but doesn't see her. She departs with her team.

Nymanne finds herself in a tunnel beneath the silos. She doesn't understand their purpose and infiltrates the dark passage with caution, with Roísín walking closely behind her, bow at the ready. They hear voices approaching and slip into the darkness.

VOICE

"Demolish these silos even by force!" Said an angry male voice.
VOICE 2
Master we have set them on fire, using the magic powder, as you have instructed. Should the villagers attempt to put the fire out, they will perish.

VOICE
So let them perish then, in the name of God!

Both leave before they can distinguish the two female forms hiding in the shadows. Nymanne pauses silently, awaiting their departure, then signals to Roísín to retreat. At the tunnel entrance, they are surprised by a guard brandishing his sword.

NYMANNE
"No witnesses" she commands quietly.

Roisin aims directly for the head. The arrow pierces through and he falls silently to the ground.

Upon exiting, Nymanne calmly glances at his black robe and turban.

NYMANNE
"Scythians", she whispers to Roísín, bewildered.

They both exit the scene and infiltrate the forest.

Scene 3

Edmund was careful to avoid the family palace. He knew that Nymanne often wandered far from the palace. She frequently did so as a child, as he and his siblings were often sent out by their mother to go looking for her. He sees her standing motionless upon the cliffs edge. Her back turned to him. He moves in stealthily behind her.

EDMUND

"Nymanne." He whispers almost inaudibly.

She knows who it is. Winces painfully. But doesn't turn back towards him. He can see her shrugging faintly.

EDMUND

Nymanne. I have come to speak with you for I know that you are friendly with the witch folk. I have seen you almost floating while seated under the trees, caught in some dark slumber. I know you know of them, Nymanne. I pray you ask them what has befallen Morrìgan. She walks in the night as though bewitched; her eyes closed and wanders blindly to the dark lake. She labours at night, as she tries to empty the lake of its water, sometimes digging in with her nails in a silent scream until her hands bleed.

Nymanne smiles almost to herself still contemplating the distant moors. The wind howls in anger lifting her hair in snake like waves. She does not turn his way. And keeps her back steadfastly turned to him.

EDMUND

Nymanne please I need your help. Tell me how to fix her.

NYMANNE

Dear brother, years of not speaking to one another or the rest of your kin, and these are the first words you utter to me? You have renounced me in public as your sister, without warning and without any sign of hostility between us. You made your decision then Edmund, I suggest you commit to it now. These are my words for you. Now kindly leave me in peace.

He begins to retract silently.

NYMANNE

One last thing.

He stops to listen.

NYMANNE

"People often fight the demons of their own making. Until it consumes them completely." She says ominously, her back still turned to him.

EDMUND

What does that mean?

NYMANNE

You shall know soon enough.

Scene 4

KING CONCHOBAR

What right have you to enter my dominion without warning or invitation? I am the King here!

ENAREES

You will do well to remember your place old man! Do not forget who has placed you on that chair, even while you are old and decrepit and your people do not respect you.

KING CONCHOBAR

His voice lowers in pitch, though still livid and trembling "I would have ascended to the throne with or without you".

Enarees shakes with convulsions of uncontrollable laughter.

ENAREES

Would you have ascended whilst you are sleeping? Or would your blind worshippers have carried you here?

KING CONCHOBAR

"I am their God", he whispers almost inaudibly.

Enarees laughs, his voice echoing through the great hall with a deafening cacophony.

ENAREES

"You are nothing old man! Now rise." He commands, with great disdain.

KING CONCHOBAR

"Why must I rise?" He mumbles trembling.

ENAREES

I said rise!

Conchobar rises almost immediately, completely dumbstruck. His strength quickly fails him, and he falls to the floor. His guards rush to help him, bewildered.

ENAREES

"Attempt to come to his aid, and you move at your own peril!" he threatens menacingly.

The guards return quietly to their place of vigil.

Enarees sits on the throne, his thorax expanding proudly as he surveys his dominion. He looks down at Conchobar, his almost lifeless body writhing beneath him.

ENAREES

"It appears you have finally remembered your place." He says sardonically. "Now that we have that sorted, listen carefully to the plan you must execute down to the last letter."

Scene 5

Nymanne enters in haste trying to pass the halls unseen and slips into her chambers. She finds her mother standing at her door.

LADY IGRAINE

My word Nymanne wherever have you been? You are late for the ball! How will we ever get you ready in time?

NYMANNE

"Apologies mother," she sighs exasperatedly, "I had gotten distracted with some chores."

LADY IGRAINE

You got distracted, doing what may I ask? Of course, you don't answer me. You throw some dim excuse for your whereabouts. This is not suitable for a lady. A woman's place is...

NYMANNE

"Mother please, I beg of you, could we refrain from the theatricals of a woman's place, just this once? You care only to demean women and yourself in the process. This truly baffles me, how one can wish to systematically think of oneself as inferior." She looks vaguely inquisitive, though assumes the question to be rhetorical, as it is often dismissed without a second thought.

LADY IGRAINE

I am doing what is best for you! While you are out galivanting in the late hours of the night, trying to create a world that simply does not exist! You need to understand our reality: a woman simply cannot exist without a man. I am doing my utmost to secure a good match for you. Given your predicament, it is no small feat.

NYMANNE

My predicament! Is this how you choose to refer to a mother with children? Is that predicament so terrible mother? What about the cruel predicament I was in before leaving that hell of an existence?

Her mother draws a blank and remains static, caught in a vapid silence.

NYMANNE

Oh of course. After all these years you still don't believe me! Much like my sister, you stood against me. You said my words were lies, that my pain was lies!

LADY IGRAINE

You should not have left him. A woman can make do with the lot that is given her. A woman causes a man to tip on either side of the scale. You were not patient in manipulating that man to your will.

Nymanne feels nauseated by the words. Those words that should never be uttered.

NYMANNE

Enough. I will get dressed now mother and go to this ball of yours, if it means acquiring a semblance of peace. I refuse to ever speak of this again. Now pray, leave me to get ready.

As soon as the door closes, she begins to inhale deeply, mustering her strength. She proceeds to paint her face half-heartedly, like donning a mask, desperately attempting to veil her disgust. She practices smiling courteously in the mirror several times, before exiting her chambers.

Scene 6

The King's palace is grand and lavishly decorated for the ball. The sumptuous ornaments lie in stark contrast with the poverty of his Kingdom, that has been made to bleed through his endless greed and devious acts. The guests behave as though they lived in the happiest of times, surrounded by opulence and wealth. They are oblivious to the famine that prevails beyond these gated walls.

LADY IGRAINE

"This will be our opportunity to show you to the court." She exclaims, with barely contained glee.

NYMANNE

I am not a debutante mother, I am a divorcée, does the court not look down upon such unworthy specimens of society? You have no need to treat me like a show horse. I am finished with that disparaging chapter of my existence, as a woman, in this godforsaken land.

LADY IGRAINE

Hush child! I have pulled many strings to get you an invitation to this ball.

NYMANNE

You needn't have pulled any strings mother. I get an invitation to this ball every year, in a special request to read for the King.

LADY IGRAINE

Gracious me! Then why have you not attended the ball with your father and I before this?

NYMANNE

I will not read for this orange tinted buffoon! What poetry and praise could I write for such a decaying specimen of poor leadership?

LADY IGRAINE

"Silence! Do you wish us all to be sent to the dungeons?" she sighs, "I am certainly glad you are not reading tonight; a man does not care for a woman who speaks her mind. We need to show you and find you a husband."

NYMANNE

Show Evá, she has plenty of show for both of us combined, furthermore, she loves to make a grand entrance.

LADY IGRAINE

Your sister is already married.

NYMANNE

"Perhaps we could set aside lucky number three, to be made use of at a later date." She chuckles.

LADY IGRAINE

Quiet child! Here comes a suitor now. I pray you behave yourself.

NYMANNE

"If it pleases you mother, I shall pretend to be someone else entirely." She replies sarcastically.

LADY IGRAINE

"Very well." She smiles, "Now you are truly learning the value of my teachings."

Nymanne sighs in despair. She spots a large red-haired, bearded man, of tall stature, heading their way. Very broad, a little opulent around the waistline, while the height certainly had its merits. He was rather formidable.

AIDAN

My lady, if I may steal your daughter for a dance?

LADY IGRAINE

By all means, dear sir.
He looks to Nymanne excitedly and draws her to the centre of the
ballroom as the music plays.

AIDAN

My lady, I am an avid reader of your work. I have attended many
such balls in the hope of hearing you read.

NYMANNE

"Well, that is certainly unexpected", she thinks to herself.

AIDAN

I was very pleasantly surprised that you have chosen to forego a
pen name.

NYMANNE

I have no use for pen names. If anyone should feel offended by
my being a woman, then they should avoid reading my work al-
together.

AIDAN

I very much agree. Why should intelligent women be relegated
to the back corners of society, if they happen to possess such an
intellect as to shine on their own light? Though that thought has
garnered much negative response from my father, I must admit.

NYMANNE

Your father is not fond of women?

AIDAN

He is fond of them when they know their place.

NYMANNE

Their place?

AIDAN

He laughs nervously, "His words, not mine, I assure you."

NYMANNE

"You obviously have a very singular mind, and yet you seem very affected by your father", she says, almost thinking out loud.

Aidan halts suddenly, and steps away from the dance floor.

AIDAN

"My lady I must take leave of you. Though I assure you, we shall meet again", he bows and kisses her hand.

NYMANNE

I should not have stepped out of bounds. I am sorry.

He departs in haste. Nymanne watches him walk away and begins to turn to make her own exit, when a hand grabs firmly at her arm.

BLAINE

Leaving so soon? I was hoping to make your acquaintance.

He was tall, slim, almost transparently white, with blond hair falling on the sides of his temples. Evidently good looking, but strikingly overdressed, and shining incandescently, much like a peacock.

She attempts to break free from his ever-tightening grip.
NYMANNE
Yes, I have a rather urgent matter to attend to.

BLAINE
Could I convince you to stay perhaps, and walk with me a while?

NYMANNE
"Perhaps I would, if you were to let go of me Sir." She stresses firmly, looking down at where his hand remained.

He lets go of her, almost reluctantly.

BLAINE
Forgive me, wherever are my manners? I was waiting for that dreadful fellow to leave. And here we are. Shall we walk to the balcony?

NYMANNE
"If you wish." She sighs attempting to tame her frustration with this entire evening. She was rather exasperated with this person as well, she did however, prefer to avoid the future reprimands of her mother.

BLAINE
What a glorious evening indeed! I wanted to ask you my Lady, I have noticed you seldom attend these balls?

NYMANNE
I do not much care to be in the presence of a large crowd of people.

BLAINE

Well, you can't say that lovely lady, it gave me a chance to make your charming acquaintance at last.

NYMANNE

"Well thank you, that is very kind of you." She smiles, trying to put herself at ease.

After a seemingly endless amount of small banter, with no real depth to the conversation, she grows very weary, and wishes this evening would swiftly draw to an end.

NYMANNE

Shall we return to the ball? I am certain my mother will be looking for me.

BLAINE

"I am certain that she is not dear lady, after all, you are with me, the Earl of Clare", he explains rather pompously.

NYMANNE

"Goodness me, well, there it is", she thinks to herself, rolling her eyes in agony.

NYMANNE

Of course, of course. Nonetheless, I think we must make our way inside, shall we?

She enters swiftly, without awaiting his reply. She attempts to worm her way through the crowd in order to avoid him, but her oversized evening gown prevents her from doing so. He grabs her by the arm as though in full possession of her. She grows increasingly weary of his grasp and contemplates a rather ag-

gressive manoeuvre that would subdue his enthusiasm.
LADY IGRAINE
"Earl Clare, what a pleasant surprise! I see you have met my daughter?" She beams.

BLAINE
"Yes, we have become rather closely acquainted, in fact dear Lady if I may ask your permission to..."

The entire ball freezes, the silence is almost deafening, as everyone stands to a halt, suspended in time and motion. Nymanne trembles uncontrollably. It has taken all of her strength to defer this moment in time. She doesn't know if she had even managed to utter the sacred words. Had she perhaps said them in her mind? She needed to make a swift exit, before her strength begins to wane. And then suddenly, a lone figure smiles at her across the ballroom, standing amidst the suspended crowd. There is almost an aura of light around him, in stark contrast with the dark stillness of the crowd.

He begins to walk towards her, a devilish smile marking his face, slightly tilted to one side. He seems very amused by what has taken place. The lights of the evening somehow act to highlight his presence more strikingly, while the rest of the crowd remains shrouded in darkness. He is tall, with grey hair and a shortly trimmed white beard, while his dark moustache contrasted with the rest of his facial hair, and dark eyebrows highlighted his piercing eyes. He continues to walk determinedly towards her, his steps well measured and weighted with confidence. He has a singular aura, almost radiating with an unseen force. Her heart begins to pound uncontrollably.

NYMANNE

"Why hasn't he been frozen like the rest of them? How is he now walking towards me? Who is this man? Am I creating this moment in my mind? Move. You must move now!" She thinks to herself, dumbstruck, as she shakes herself from her daze.

She manages to tear herself away. How long did this moment last? A minute? An hour? It all felt timeless, as though they were the only ones there. She knew her spell would not last for very long now. She succeeds, albeit clumsily, in making her escape, before the court could resume its' animated activity, oblivious to the events that have just unfolded.

Scene 7

She did not sleep well that night. Troubled by the events of the ball. Disturbed by who she had pretended to be, in order to please her mother, in her desperate efforts to silence the constant flow of reprimands and criticism. She was still haunted by that man's smile, the only one who had been impervious to her enchanting spell. Perhaps she had floated out of herself in a vision, and perhaps it had only been a dream.

She travels beyond the mirror, through a dimly lit hallway edged with mirrors. She is submerged in darkness, enveloped in a flowing white gown, like that of the heroines of her childhood dreams. The mirrors have no reflection; the faces have been erased by their maker. The gown floats behind her, erasing the wake of her footsteps, flowers are woven into the strands of her hair. This is the return, and from this return all things shall be born anew. This is the ritual of childhood, where vows of innocence are made. Flowers slowly appear in the mirrors that act as windows to open fields of lush vegetation, with planted daisies and flowing meadows. It is the rebirth of magic and endless possibilities. It is the genesis, the dream. Her sisters, the ladies of Avalon stand before her. She smiles and touches the face of the woman in the lake, the woman who had held her captive all these years, erasing the teardrops as they swelled and overflowed from the eyes of her reflection.

NYAMNNE

I am no longer you. I am no longer silent. And so long as I am given life upon this earth, the child within me shall never die.

Her magical sister Calliope, approaches her, and softly touches her shoulder. She gestures silently, her eyes communicating her words, for in dreams, the souls never speak. She leads Nymanne through a narrow clearing in the thick dark forest. The dense branches slowly condense into lush walls. There is a light at the end of the darkness. They are in a narrow hallway, proceeding silently towards the light, that shimmers in the distance, almost walking in procession. After what seems like an eternity, they reach a doorway. The light inside the chamber is blinding, one that is beyond this world.

NYMANNE

I know what I am destined for.

She enters the light. It is almost frightening in its intensity. In the midst of the light, a lone figure sits kneeling in prayer, with a bright aura surrounding her. Her eyes are closed. Her dark hair is tied neatly and parted at the middle. She has crimson lipstick, that lies in striking contrast to her white complexion. She wears a blue gown that spreads in a circle of reverence around her. Nymanne is bemused by this otherworldly sight. The woman opens her eyes suddenly, in a heartbeat. She is staring directly at her, into her soul. All Nymanne remembers are her eyes. A close up of her black beautifully highlighted eyes.

As she awakens, her heart races frantically.

NYMANNE
"Something has happened." She says to herself, panting.

She stands at the window of her chambers, as dusk begins to rise. As she had feared, she begins to hear the cries of the sparrowhawk. Only this time the hawk was perched on her windowsill. She carries him on her fingertips, caressing his plumage affectionately.

NYMANNE
"Have you come to comfort me my friend?" She asks, smiling sadly. "You needn't worry. I have already been warned. Go to them. I shall meet you there."

She releases the bird in flight, yet it continues to roam above her windowsill, as though in wait for her.

NYMANNE
Horus! Be gone! Return to Maeve!

But the bird does not leave.

KAY
Mother, what is Horus doing here so early? Must you leave again so soon?

NYMANNE

Indeed, my love. I must tend to urgent matters. I'm so sorry I woke you, go back to sleep.

KAY

What shall I tell grandfather, if he should question me on the reason for your absence?

NYMANNE

Tell him what we always do, that I tended to the fields on our lands, working with the villagers.

KAY

Please be careful mother.

NYMANNE

I will my glorious love. Do not worry.

She kisses him softly, caressing his hair as though to gather strength, for what she senses will be an ominous day. She jumps to the nearest branch on the windowsill, climbs down the tree, and heads to the dark forest.

Scene 8

It was the dawn of light, and the coloured sky brought her no comfort that morning. She hurries through the open fields and infiltrates the forest. What should have been a quiet morning was filled with wild shrieks. At first, she believes it to be a creature that is dying, but when she sees her Amazons pacing in despair, she begins to fear the worst.

NYMANNE

What is it Roìsin? Where is Maeve?

ROÌSIN

It's Maeve my lady. She came back from the village this morning, shrieking like a crazed animal and striking her sword on the tree trunk near the lake. We tried to talk to her with no result. She could not even see us. She even pushed me away when I tried to approach her! Now she has replaced the sword with her hands. They are bleeding but she will not stop striking the trunk. There is so much blood, that I know not what to do!

They head towards the lake. Maeve writhes in agony, punching the trunk, her hands bloodied and torn. She continues like an enraged beast, as though enchanted by a magic spell. Finding no relief to her pain, she begins to tear the tree bark with her bare hands.

NYMANNE

Maeve stop!

She runs towards her, Maeve doesn't see her, blinded by her rage. When Nymanne attempts to move her away, Maeve tries to punch her. She barely misses, and Nymanne must push her away aggressively. Maeve looks up. She is wakened from her daze, and begins to pant hysterically, staring blankly at all those around her.

NYMANNE

Everyone please, leave us.

ROÌSIN

My Lady no.

NYMANNE

I said leave now Roìsin! Everyone must leave, please.

The Amazons leave the lake and head back into the forest.

NYMANNE

You can choose to strike me or talk to me. Either way Maeve, I'm not leaving. Do you hear me?

Maeve collapses near the water's edge, and weeps. Nymanne goes to comfort her. She embraces her, swaying her from side to side, waiting for her violent cries to cease. For a long time, they stare silently at the water.

NYMANNE

What is it Maeve? You can trust me.

MAEVE

Luana is dead. They have killed her.

NYMANNE

That girl from the village we once helped. Who has killed her?

MAEVE

"The so-called Guardians of Morality." She says spitting out the words in disgust.

NYMANNE

Who are they? Why did they kill her?

MAEVE

They took her away in the night, while she was crossing the fields back to her home. They told her family it was considered indecent for her not to cover her hair. That men would be tempted by this. They said they needed to "correct" her.

NYMANNE

Correct her? Those beasts. What do they know of morality? They hide behind the manufactured laws of the new religion, created by men, in order to impose their dominion over women. Those evil monsters!

MAEVE

"They brought her body back this morning, she was unconscious. They couldn't wake her from her sleep. And then she... she..." Maeve sobs.

NYMANNE

Maeve... Did you love her?

MAEVE

What? No, she was one of the women we helped. I'm only sorry we could not save her from these animals.

NYMANNE

Maeve, you have always been my source of support and strength. You are more than a sister to me. Let me be there for you, my friend. It is not unholy to love. Do not let anyone convince you otherwise. Did you love her my friend?

Maeve weeps uncontrollably. After what seems like an eternity, she finally reveals her story, with the only person she knew she could trust.

MAEVE

"We used to meet in the dead of night, when no one could see us. She would often sneak out of her home and meet me in our secret cave. She told me that her village of Bodmin had slowly been taken over by those so-called guardians of morality. The Kings' army never intervened to stop them, and they often resorted to violence when they were opposed by the villagers. Lately, they had imposed a curfew. I didn't know she was risking her life to come and meet me." She sobs, "It is my fault she is dead." She beats her head with her hands in anguish.

Nymanne reaches out to stop Maeve's hand.

NYMANNE

"Maeve stop, stop, please stop. Do not blame yourself for the cowardly actions of these monsters. We shall avenge her death. I promise you this."

Maeve continues to beat herself.

NYMANNE

"You have trusted me with your secret, and now I shall share mine."
She touches the earth with her left hand, and with her right hand she touches Maeve, who continues to beat herself blindly. Nymanne goes into a trance like state, while chanting the sacred words.
"Shoko rei, shoko rei, hon sha ze sho nen."

Ripples of energy are created at the centre of the lake, they move towards Nymanne and Maeve. When they reach the shore, they convert to droplets, that move in unison towards Maeve, gently wrapping themselves around her body, carrying her in slight suspension above the ground. Nymanne continues in her trance, chanting the words and touching the earth to seek out its healing powers. The water begins to glow, as it transfers the energy of the earth to Maeve.

"Release your pain my sister. Sleep now. You shall feel better in the night."

ACT III
The Mist

Scene 1

It is the night of that same day. Maeve sleeps in her tent, suspended in the trees, deep in the dark forest in the Amazonian hideout. Several Amazon guards stand vigil.

NYMANNE

Awaken dear Maeve.

MAEVE

How long have I been asleep?

NYMANNE

"You have slept throughout the entire day." She says, stroking her hair, as she did her children's. "It gave me enough time to see the children and devise a plan." She says with a knowing smile.

MAEVE

A plan for what?

NYMANNE

Revenge. We shall avenge your dear Luana, and all the poor souls these vile beasts have persecuted through their false ideology. Her death will not be in vain; I promise you that.

Maeve smiles. She was confident that whatever Nymanne sets her mind to, she can achieve. Nymanne knew the only way Maeve could find peace was through justice being served.

MAEVE

I know what you have done to heal me.

NYMANNE

And that shall remain our secret. I am trusting you, my friend. You have always stood by me.

MAEVE

And I shall always stand by you, with all of my heart. I believe in you, Nymanne. With these powers you have shown me, I believe in you even more! Imagine all the people we can heal! Why do you hide it from the Amazons? They are your sisters as I am yours. Tell me, what other powers do you possess?

NYMANNE

"I am still learning to discover my power, and my strengths. It is like an awakening. When I was a young girl, I was consistently convinced by my family, my mother, that a woman is only destined for certain things. And out of love for my father and wishing to earn his love, I thought I must remain true to their ideal of what a woman is meant to be. The power and urge within me had always seeped through, however. Many times, it fought to break free, violently consuming me at times, particularly in dreams, as I often sought to repress it. The more I repressed, the more I felt the urge to harm myself. This need that I felt was left unfulfilled. In order to belong, I felt I needed to be other than myself. And yet, despite all my efforts, I never managed to belong. I was never accepted by them." She sheds a silent tear.

MAEVE

You need never have conformed to such a mediocre role!

NYMANNE

"Yes, I know that now. But their love was conditional. And so, I always tried to earn their love, growing up. I decided long ago, that to conform was death for me. Ever since that time, my powers have grown. More so after becoming a mother, perhaps my powers grew in a bid to protect those I love the most in this world." She smiles, looking into the distance.

MAEVE

Tell me please, what other powers do you possess?

NYMANNE

I can halt time. Only briefly. The more beings there are in one space, the more I am drained of my energy afterwards. There is a price for using one's power Maeve. Not in healing, for that is giving. I healed you with the powers of the earth, energy that is ever present all around us. Humans are so lost. They seek the wrong kind of power, through accumulating armies and wealth. Whilst the true power that has been offered to us is abundant in nature. An infinite energy offered to us in order to heal and create.

MAEVE

Who has taught you this?

NYMANNE

Most I have discovered for myself or have appeared in times of crisis. Many years ago, I had a dream, I was flying over a desert landscape. It felt so vividly real Maeve, I could smell the air around me, the wind as it swept my hair. I arrived at a cave entrance. There were many such houses carved into the stone, with columns marking the entrances.

MAEVE

What far off lands are those, what in the name of Modron is a desert?

NYMANNE

Imagine the sand we find on the beach but extending into great plains, plains that have mounds that act like waves.

MAEVE

"Your words can certainly help to conjure dreams Nymanne." She smiles softly, contemplating that alternate world.

NYMANNE

In this dream, there were druids, they were cloaked, and spoke to me through the power of their minds.

MAEVE

"I thought druids only taught their fellow man." She said sarcastically.

NYMANNE

"Perhaps that is why they visited me in dreams." They smile to one another knowingly. "I was to pass several tests, in every level, a new spiritual awakening could be acquired. I had to overcome many trials in that cave Maeve, in what felt like an eternity, climbing steps carved in the stone above an abyss, and fighting off wild imaginary beasts. But on the seventh level, I needed only to cross an expanse of water. At first, I doubted it could be so simple. But as I leaped towards the final crossing, deadly spirits overpowered me, they whistled loudly in my mind, in deafening cries. What was indeed worse than that experience, was the dreadful sensation of being stripped of my very being, of feeling my soul slowly ebbing away, and being overwhelmed with a feeling of coldness, as though overcome by death itself."

MAEVE

What happened then?

NYMANNE

I pleaded with the druids to save me. My mind was pierced by the shrieking sounds, like a deafening scream that broke the barriers of my sanity. Voices whispered to me that I was not yet ready.

MAEVE

And then you were sent to face them?

NYMANNE

Then I awakened. Completely haunted by that experience. But with the knowledge of a new language, and several powerful spells. Do you believe it was real?

MAEVE

Yes, I do.

NYMANNE

How do you know?

MAEVE

There are many mysteries in this world we know not of.

Scene 2

The Amazons are huddled and seated in a circle. A campfire burns, a full moon lights the sky and rustles with the burning amber. Nymanne stands in the centre, her muscular frame and wild brown mane is highlighted by the wildfire blazing behind her. She feels empowered by it.

NYMANNE

Remember who you are. They have taken your freedom! They have deprived you of your children! And meanwhile, they have convinced you that as women, you must always be told what to do!

The women collectively make the hawk cry in retaliation to the injustices of this world.

NYMANNE

And now, if that wasn't enough, they have created the greatest perversion ever to mark the history of man! They call themselves Guardians of morality! And while they preach morality, and pretend to uphold it, they steal, they kill!

Maeve grieves silently, a single tear flows down her cheek, while she attempts to contain the tremor overcoming her body.

NYMANNE

Tonight, while they sleep, we will take our power back. We will teach them what it is to have remained hidden, like they have forced us to be. Tonight, they shall die at the invisible hand of vindication! Tonight, we shall reclaim... our freedom!

The hawk cries become impassioned as one. One voice. One strength. One heartbeat.

NYMANNE

"We will lurk in the shadows until we can all rise in the sun! And believe me. One day we... shall... rise!" She draws her fist up as though she was harnessing the power of the moon.

Scene 3

Nymanne stands with Maeve. They look upon Dosmary pool with reluctance. The light of the full moon flickers on the still surface.

MAEVE

Are you certain that you wish to do this?

NYMANNE

My dream before I came to see you. I think I know what it means. I think the time is now. We must free our sisters, and this sword will surely help us in fulfilling our destiny. It is time. I am now certain of this.

MAEVE

"I am with you. If the sword does not yield. I beg you return to the surface. Otherwise, I shall have to come rescue you. And you know how I hate doing that." She chuckles jokingly.

NYMANNE

"You have always stood by me Maeve. I pray I shall never give you reason to save me. But if you must, then do not let me drown." Nymanne jokes apprehensively. She enters the water, and turns to Maeve. "I am happy I am no longer doing this alone. That you are sharing in my secret." They smile knowingly to one another.

Nymanne enters the dark mysterious water of the lake. She feels its hold upon her. She moves forward to its centre, and suddenly panics as she is violently pulled downwards, letting out a wild cry as she disappears completely below the surface, as though overpowered by some invisible beast. Maeve becomes agitated at the sight of this and considers rescuing her. She moves to the centre of the lake but can detect nothing in the bleak darkness of the water. She dives helplessly in the lake, several times, with no clear direction.

Nymanne continues to be pulled violently downwards, she scrambles to resist, as the air is almost drained from her lungs. She then decides to stop resisting, gives in and is now gently pulled to the bed of the lake, where the sword rests, as though in wait for her. This time when she attempts to grab it, she finds no resistance, it lights up, almost pulsating with her heartbeat. She feels they are now one and senses a unison with the water around her. She is at peace, the water so silent she almost wishes she can remain there forever. As she begins to drift into the sweet release of sleep, the sword she now holds in her right arm begins to propel her upwards and pulls her to the surface. She takes her first breath, expelling a loud scream as she did so, as though born again.

In the far distance, a man hides in the forest entrance, unseen. He wears a cloak and the hood above his head shields him from wandering eyes. He watches stealthily. When Nymanne resurfaces, he breathes a sigh of relief and smiles with that same knowing smile of the evening when they first met, in all her burgeoning, magical splendour.

MERLIN

She is ready.

Scene 4

The Amazons group around Nymanne in the dark forest, for one final briefing before they embark on their mission.

NYMANNE

My ladies, I will need all your strength this very night. What we are about to undertake will not be easy on any of us. Tonight, we must do the unthinkable. Tonight, we must kill mercilessly, against those who have perpetrated many crimes and destroyed many lives. Do not feel pity towards them when they are sleeping. Even in dreams,they dream of the very evils they have committed and take pleasure in doing so. Do not feel compassion towards them, for they are inhuman. Tonight, we avenge the countless lives they have taken, at whim and without justification. Tonight, you will witness things you might not comprehend. All I can reveal to you is that the forces of nature will be with us, and they shall guide us in restoring the balance of power, and destroying those that personify perversions against nature, against the heart of this earth. Mother Modron grant you the strength to remain steadfast no matter what you may see. That is your mission. Heed my words, no matter what you may see tonight, be steadfast in your mission, do not waiver.

MAEVE

We need our stealth armour tonight. Everyone disperse and be prepared on my order!

NYMANNE

"This night will be hard on them." She shudders.

MAEVE

Why must you feel pity for these monsters? The women will derive great pleasure in killing them and ridding the world of their evil. Many of these so-called guardians of morality have persecuted one of their kin. Many mirror the anger and despair that I feel. Many seek vengeance and retribution.

NYMANNE

It is not only about the killing Maeve. What I am about to do, will help us all, but it shall also mark us forever. I must protect them; to do so I must do the unthinkable. You should know Maeve, that after the clock strikes twelve, it shall be the 31st of October.

MAEVE

And what if it is?

NYMANNE

October 31st marks the day of Samhain, when the border between the two worlds disappears and it is possible for people to enter the otherworld, so too the beings from the otherworld can visit ours.

MAEVE

That is why you stalled this mission by ten days. It was not only to retrieve the sword. Did you really require a full moon to retrieve it?

NYMANNE

The moon is at its optimum energy when it is full, I needed the comfort of its nurturing light to guide me.

MAEVE

Why could you not have revealed the truth to me, as you have done all else thus far?

NYMANNE

Tonight, I am afraid of what I must do. I did not wish for you to carry that same burden. Tonight, the dead shall rise. And while one cycle ends, another shall begin. It will mark a rebirth for us all.

MAEVE

Then I understand why you chose not to tell me. And I am with you.

NYMANNE

As agreed, you will head the team that will guard the entrance and operate on ground level. While Roìsin and her archers will climb to the upper strongholds. I cannot perform what I must in the presence of the others. I shall remain hidden. Do not allow them to come looking for me. I shall provide cover for you. Do not be shaken by what you shall see.

MAEVE

If they can provide us with guidance, then let the dead rise. I will be ready, as will the rest of my team.

Scene 5

The Amazons take their positions. The first team is sent to man the grounds and disable any guard at the entrances. Arrows fly, and swords silently cut throats in the dark of night, while bodies are swiftly removed.

Maeve and her team circle the fortress entrance, while Roìsins' team launch the ropes on neighbouring trees and link their pitons to strongholds, and crevasses in the walls.

Nymanne watches them from a distance, and hidden in a clearing beneath the trees, she powerfully plants her sword next to the roots of an oak tree, the sacred tree. She goes into a trance like state, breathing strongly, and expels the powers within her, merging with her sword and the roots beneath her feet. On the sword, the letters inscribed *Gabh mi suas agus tilg air falbh mi* begin to pulsate with light. They translate to *take me up and cast me away*, as no one person is ever meant to own unbounded power. It is only to be weilded in a time of need.

NYMANNE

Mala Revelentur. Let the sacred earth open its gates between our two worlds. Mala Releventur. Let the Great Mother reclaim its due and correct these human transgressions. *Mala Revelentur.*

The earth begins to crack beneath her feet, as the roots spread to reveal a great abysmal void. She does not waver. Holding onto her sword and chanting the sacred words, another four times to reach the powerful number seven.

A mist begins to rise around the Guardians fortress, shrouding it completely. Maeve continues to hold, awaiting a signal. From within the fortress, one silent male scream pierces the silence. It is followed by another scream, and another. Until the entire fortress is plagued by wailing male screams, all shrieking hysterically in unison. Maeve gives the signal to Roìsin. The Amazons send many piercing arrows through the window, killing everyone in the first room, and are perplexed to find no resistance. Within, the screams continue to rise. Roìsin and her team proceed inwards and penetrate the first room through the window, while Maeve and her team enter from below. The women attack the guardians who are blind to them, looking only upon an invisible presence before them, shrieking wildly as though a witness to a rise from the dead. It is almost painful to kill a helpless madman, consumed by some imaginary vision, but the women were warned, and they persist in their quest, unyielding.

Maeve circles the perimeter, checking for any survivors. She climbs the steps to the upper tower and finds one chief guardian, in a large room at the top of the fortress, seemingly their grand master, dressed in richly robes and sitting upright on his bed, shrieking loudly, looking unto an invisible presence that terrifies him to his very core.

MASTER OF THE GUARDIANS

"I didn't mean to! I didn't mean to hurt you! An example needed to be made! I needed to set an example! Stop!" He shields his face. "Don't hurt me! Stop!"

Maeve begins to understand. It is one of his victims, confronting him. she follows his gaze, and turns her eyes in the same direction. Then, as though in an apparition through the mist, a young girl of sixteen appears, beautiful with dark hair, with a fringe covering her forehead and large expressive eyes with red full lips. Her nose is shattered and when she turns to Maeve, she can see that the right side of her skull is deeply fractured as well. The apparition lunges angrily at the guardian master who shrieks hysterically, as though experiencing an inner burning, with every stab of her transluscent hands. She strikes him with her fist time and time again, as he continues to screech helplessly. Maeve watches in disbelief. Finally, when she is done, she turns to Maeve with a pleading look in her innocent eyes. Maeve understanding her request, plunges the sword deep into the guardian's heart. With her eyes closed, she imagines Luana at her side while she is avenging her.

The mist disappears, as the light of dawn paints the sky. The fortress is silent once more.

Scene 6

MAEVE

"I saw that young girl Nymanne. That poor young girl." She shudders uncontrollably.

NYMANNE

I am sorry you had to see that. I did not really know what you would or would not be able to see.

MAEVE

None of the other Amazons saw the victims, thank the Gods. They only saw the fear in the guardians' eyes. And that was enough to send chills down their spine. I could see that she was at peace now, that young girl, as I imagine my Luana would be." She sighs longingly. "I wish I could have seen her, just one last time."

NYMANNE

"I'm sure she was with you. It is better you don't remember her that way, as a victim. I must go to my children Maeve. Make sure the Amazons are not distraught this evening. Take care of them. I will see you very soon." Gathering her strength, she struggles not to collapse, attempting to control her body as it tremors from sheer exhaustion.

MAEVE

Nymanne what is it? You are not well!

NYMANNE

The spell has taken its toll on me. Linking the two worlds demands a just sacrifice, so balance can be restored. I offered the executioners to their victims. It was the right form of retribution, and justice was served. I will be well Maeve. Do not worry. I must go now.

Nymanne makes her way through the forest, and when she feels she is completely alone, she allows herself to collapse on the floor and looks to the moon, sobbing uncontrollably, quietly hugging herself as she did so.

VOICE

Nymanne.

Nymanne is startled by the male voice, behind her, whispering softly to her. She fears she has imagined it and refuses to look back.

VOICE

"Nymanne." Murmurs the voice.

She turns hesitantly, wielding her sword in defence of a potential ambush. She discerns a lone shrouded figure, coming out of the darkness, like an apparition. He slowly removes the hood of his cloak, revealing powerful eyes that overwhelm her.

NYMANNE

"It is you!" She gasps in disbelief, taking one step back, almost out of breath.

MERLIN

Yes.

NYMANNE

"What are you doing here? How did you find me?" She asks,

pointing her sword at him.

MERLIN

"I have been watching you since the ball. Since you halted time. Since you bewitched me." He smiles.

NYMANNE

My spell did not seem to have any effect on you then.

MERLIN

"Not the spell itself, but I was enchanted, nonetheless." He continues to smile softly at her, as she slowly lowers her sword.

NYMANNE

Who are you?

MERLIN

I am Merlin, some like to call me Merlin the Wizard. We have much in common you and I, more than you could ever imagine. I sensed I was to meet someone like you, I dreamed it, though I never envisioned your face. Nymanne, I am here to help you.

NYMANNE

Thank you, but I have all the help I could need.

She struggles to pick herself up from the floor, wavering as she did so, and attempts to walk off, clumsily dragging her sword behind her. He rushes to help her, gently supporting her arm, while allowing her to lean on him. This was in such contrast with that buffoon who had grabbed her arm that night at the ball, she thinks. She reluctantly allows him to help her, not accepting to lean fully upon him.

MERLIN

You often rush to save others, Nymanne, but tell me, who is saving you?

NYMANNE

"I do not need saving". She shudders, holding back her tears.

MERLIN

We all need saving Nymanne. Let's agree to help each other. Forgive me if my words have offended you.

NYMANNE

What help do you require of me?

MERLIN

That sword that yields to you, do you know that in time, it is destined for another?

NYMANNE

Yes, I felt it. I felt I was meant to carry it, until a time where it will be called by the one it was destined for. I asked the sword to help me tonight, much needed to be accomplished., I needed all the help I could get.

MERLIN

In time the sword will reach its destined seeker. But he who wields it, will only be given such right by you. By your grace.

NYMANNE

"By me?", she asks bewildered, "I have no notion of who that might be."

MERLIN

In due time all will be revealed.

NYMANNE

"How do I know that I can trust you?" She looks up at him over-whelmed, with childlike innocence.

He smiles knowingly, understanding that she already did.

MERLIN

"On a scale of one to ten, what are my chances that you shall one day trust me completely?" He asks playfully, trying to lighten the moment.

She thinks long and hard, attempting to control her natural urge to dismiss others and raise her protective walls.

NYMANNE

Five.

MERLIN

"Five. I will take that. If during our next encounters, I can raise that number even by one, then I shall be a happy man." He uses this distraction to carry her, as she allows herself to let go com-pletely, drifting into a deep sleep.

Scene 7

GAWAIN

Mother, please awaken. Are you not well?

Nymanne awakens to look upon her son's concerned face. She feels very disoriented. How did she get here? How did she make her way back and into her bed chambers? Was she still in her battle attire? She looks beneath the sheets and realizes that she is wearing her nightgown. She turns crimson as she recalls that Merlin had carried her here, in the dark of the night.

GAWAIN

Mother, I heard you crying in your sleep. Please tell me, what is troubling you?

NYMANNE

Do not worry my sweet love, it was only a bad dream.

GAWAIN

Mother your hands are muddy, I pray you bathe and wash them before grandfather can take notice. I informed him you were taken ill. I shall go and distract him.

NYMANNE

"Thank you, my love." Then she smiles thinking to herself, "this boy is becoming a man, it might be time to share my truth with him, it appears that he already suspects something".

Scene 8

Nymanne and Gawain lie side by side on a large branch high up in the trees surrounding the castle, they look upon the sky as the sun begins to set, turning the heavens into a crescendo of amber and crimson.

NYMANNE

Behold nature's wonders, Gawain. Mother earth has blessed us with so much, and yet mankind continues to destroy it for his own selfish greed.

GAWAIN

Are men inherently evil, mother?

NYMANNE

No, my love, they act out of fear and ignorance. Ignorance is the pathway to evil, seeking to destroy what they do not comprehend.

Horus circles above them, as though standing guard.

GAWAIN

Mother, why is Horus circling above us, instead of resting on your arm, like he always does?

Nymanne smiles knowingly, crossing her arms upon her chest.

NYMANNE

I believe Maeve has instructed him to watch over me, she knows how I would hate it if she came to check on me herself.

GAWAIN

You have long told me that Maeve was your dearest friend, but is there more to it than what you say? Why were your hands covered in mud, this morning? Why did you scream in the night during your sleep?

NYMANNE

I am sorry I have troubled you, my son. Is there something else you are not telling me? Is there something else I might have done in my sleep? Did you sneak into my room at night?

GAWAIN

I slept by your side. I couldn't possibly leave you alone mother, you were trembling uncontrollably, whispering the words *Mala Revelentur,* over and over again, relentlessly.

She silently sheds a tear; her hands begin to heat up with energy.

NYMANNE

I beg you, never speak these words again, there is so much you don't yet know.

GAWAIN

Then tell me; I am ready mother.

NYMANNE

Indeed, you are my love. There is so much evil in this world I wish to protect you from, but now I know that I cannot continue to do so forever.

GAWAIN

Is this an evil you are fighting?

NYMANNE

"How intelligent you are". She smiles warmly. "Yes, the new state of rule has laid plunder to this Kingdom, and even honest men do not see the full scale of persecution that is inflicted upon women".

GAWAIN

I understand mother, I also understand why we must shield

grandfather from ever knowing the truth. He would never understand.

NYMANNE

"No, indeed he would not, sadly. You are right. How wonderful you have grown to become, I am so infinitely proud of you, my son". She leans forward to kiss him and by doing so touches her right hand to his left arm. Suddenly, a flash of imagery floods her mind, and a knight with a sword appears before her. She pulls her hand away, perplexed. "You have had a vision."

He looks upon her startled.

GAWAIN

I do not know if it is a vision or a dream. He said he knows me. He said our futures have always been intertwined. He said you must find him, and restore what is his.

NYMANNE

When did you dream this?

GAWAIN

Last night mother. After being awakened by your screams. When I fell back to sleep next to you.

NYMANNE

"Did you speak my words?" She hesitates, "The sacred words?"

GAWAIN

I did.

She shudders and squeezes his hand feverishly.

NYMANNE

It has begun. What once was cannot be again. I did not know that you were a part of it. It is time for your training to begin my son.

GAWAIN

Who is this man mother?

NYMANNE

I do not yet know. But there is something we must deliver to him, and it seems that you will be the one to help me.

Just as she utters these words, Horus suddenly plunges downwards, screeching as he does so. Nymanne, bewildered, climbs down the tree to find the bird, moving stealthily. Her son runs swiftly ahead of her, landing on the ground in a backward flip, as he proceeds to seek out the mighty bird with his small yet muscular frame. They both move to a hidden clearing within the entrance of the forest, where the bird was last seen. They discover Horus resting on the arm of a hooded man. Nymanne initially pulls her son behind her protectively, but then realizes they are safe, as she recognizes the man standing before her.

NYMANNE

"I should have known." She thinks, "How long have you been standing here?", she asks almost accusingly, yet holding back a smile.

MERLIN

"Not long." He hesitates, smiling. "A while. All night."

Gawain stands silently next to his mother, with an inquisitive stare.

NYMANNE

You too were checking on me? I am fine! Why must everyone suddenly be checking on me? How did Horus come to you if he does not know you?

MERLIN

"I have a way of communicating with all kinds of beings. Horus was just helping me in drawing your attention." He caresses the bird as they look upon each other like old friends. The bird bows its head affectionately. "Animals can see what we do not."

NYMANNE

And yet it seems, you can see everything.

MERLIN

"Perhaps." He smiles at her.

NYMANNE

Who is the knight the sword is destined for? And why has he chosen my son to be his voice?

Merlin smiles to the boy, and winks warmly at him. Gawain smiles back, deciding to simply trust in the events unfolding before him, without question, as though comforted by an unspoken voice.

MERLIN

"Good lad". He says smilingly to Gawain.

NYMANNE

Are you communicating mentally with my son?

MERLIN

I was merely bringing comfort to him; all will be well Nymanne.
Fear not.

NYMANNE

You have not yet told me to whom the sword the lake has entrusted me with, is really destined for?

MERLIN

"Arthur." He says ominously, in an echoing whisper.

ACT IV
The Revelation

Scene 1

The wind rages along Bodmin moor, howling as it sweeps across the fens, almost uprooting the tall swept grass with its sheer power. As the torrential rain pours down relentlessly, in this dark filled night, an incomprehensible sight can be seen from afar: two lone figures, lost in the vast wildness of the moors, attempt to confront the violent storm, making their way towards Dozmary Pool.

EDMUND

Morrìgan what are you doing? Morrìgan please stop! This is madness!

The figure walks as though bewitched and continues unaffected by the man standing before her. Her blank stare indicates that she is either asleep or overcome by a deep trancelike state.

Back o'er the moor, the frozen moor,
Flies the cursed soul to Dozmary Pool.
With gleaming fangs and eyes aflame.
The pack, the pack, the hellish pack
Race by her side, yap, yap, yap –
Race by the side of the soul in pain.*

He tries to stop her to no avail, as she appears transported by an immutable force. Onwards she heads to her inevitable fate, showing no sign of a true awakening. He struggles to keep up, pulled backwards by the howling winds, as though it was a foreboding of the horrors that were to imminently unfold. Helpless and dumbstruck, he continues to follow her. He had seen her "possessed" before, but never quite so beastly in her determi-

* *The Ballad of the Haunted Moor*

nation. She resembled the walking dead, set upon a quest to destroy all that stood in her wake. Finally, she reaches the pool, and as her feet touch the water, she begins to dig mindlessly, with her bare hands, throwing the earth ashore, as though in a bid to empty the lake of its bottomless depths. Thus, she continues, echoing the sound of the winds as she howls and roars at the hopelessness of her task. Her fingers begin to bleed profusely, as the water around her slowly turns crimson. Edmund makes one final attempt to stop her, and propels her forcefully backwards, trying to shake her from her trance as he did so. She beats him down viciously as he falls helpless to the ground. Soon after, a terrifying figure hovers above him, hissing with eyes wild and her blond hair writhing in snake like strands that convolute with the wind in the night sky. He no longer recognizes her, and now only saw a maniacal creature towering above him, enraptured by the violence of the storm.

MORRÌGAN

It's mine! All mine! You can't have it! Mine do you hear me?

She returns to her quest, determined to possess the infinite depths of the lake.

Scene 2

Nymanne, Kay, Gawain and Merlin stand in the courtyard near Scone Abbey, staring intently at the forgers working relentlessly before them, as the bustle of city life noisily unfolds.

NYMANNE

Merlin, you have asked me to trust you and I have. We have travelled with you for nine days and nine nights, the children and I, all in the name of proving my faith in you. Now we stare blankly at forgers and blacksmiths. Will you please tell me, what on earth we are doing here?

MERLIN

I am waiting for something to be revealed.

NYMANNE

Ah! Speaking in prophetic code, I see! I wish you could reveal the truth to me simply, just once in direct words, before the exhaustive use of lengthy riddles.

Merlin smiles mysteriously.

MERLIN

Patience my Lady is, a talent you do not possess, though your other talents are far too numerous to recount.

Nymanne suddenly turns silent and perplexed. She could certainly gain from attaining some level of patience and poise. How is it that he knew her so well?

MERLIN

Gawain my dearest boy, would you be so kind as to check where our carriage is being held?

Gawain relieved at the distraction, wanders off in search of the carriage. He finds it abandoned without its driver, with one of the horses missing. He proceeds to find the horse tied near one of the blacksmith workshops, with one of his horseshoes removed. He approaches the horse lovingly; he adored all animals and was strongly drawn to them.

GAWAIN

"My dear Bolt, did you miss me, you gorgeous steed?" He caresses his head and hands him a carrot.

BLACKSMITH

"Can I help you my young lad?" A voice says joyfully behind him.

Gawain turns and is suddenly dumbstruck, unable to utter a word.

BLACKSMITH

What is it? Are you feeling unwell my lad?

GAWAIN

"It is you." He whispers.

The blacksmith stares attentively at the boy, trying to decipher the reason for the child's sudden reaction. Then it hits him, the memory of that face, years older, standing beside him in battle. He thought it to be merely a passing dream, of long-lost knighthood and valour.

ARTHUR

I...I dreamed you in my sleep, did you dream of me as well?

GAWAIN

"Yes. You are Arthur." Gawain mumbles, his voice almost inaudible.

The boy and the young man continue to stare intently at one another in disbelief.

ARTHUR

"How is it that you know my name?" Arthur asks, almost rhetorically

MERLIN

"Well, I see that you have made each other's acquaintance at last." He says with a paternal smile.

Nymanne stares incredulously at what she now understands to be her half-brother.

The young man feels ill at ease with all these people staring earnestly at him. He so wished this moment would come to an end.

ARTHUR

Who are you sir? I pray someone tell me what strange turn of events this is. Who is this young lad, and how is it that I have dreamed of him?

Nymanne is startled. She looks to Merlin questioningly. Did he do this? Did he plant the dream in the minds of both uncle and nephew?

MERLIN

I am not as powerful as you believe me to be, Nymanne! Now, let us focus on making the right introductions, shall we?

NYMANNE

"Shielding my mind from intrusive telepathy. That is a talent I must urgently acquire." She thinks to herself, exasperated. She nods approvingly.

MERLIN

My boy, I pray you do not panic. We have come in search of you.

This young lad has anticipated your whereabouts, in a dream, as you well know. It was a message for us to come find you.

ARTHUR

Find me? And pray, for what purpose?

MERLIN

Let us begin with gradual introductions, shall we? I am Merlin, and this strapping young lad... is your nephew.

Arthur stands aghast as though suddenly punched in the chest. He feels out of breath and lost for words by this sequential bombardment of information.

ARTHUR

My nephew? But I am an orphan... and an only child.

MERLIN

Did you know your father?

ARTHUR

Yes, my father Gorlois died in battle many years ago, when I was but a boy of two.

MERLIN

My lad, Gorlois did indeed die in battle, when he was sent to fight as a general to protect the dominion of Lord Pendragon against the Saxons, however... he is not your father.

ARTHUR

I... I don't believe you.

MERLIN

Will you accept to dine with us tonight? More will be revealed then.

Scene 3

Nymanne knocks determinedly at Merlin's door.

NYMANNE

"This time I shall get the answers I require, even if it means be-witching him, if I can even manage to bewitch a powerful wiz-ard such as he." She sighs, as though forcing herself to manifest these events in her minds' eye.

MERLIN

Are the children asleep?

NYMANNE

Yes. I lay them to sleep in their beds, they were exhausted from such an arduous journey. It didn't take them long to drift into a deep slumber.

MERLIN

I am glad. I realize this was a difficult journey for children their age.

NYMANNE

Why did you request that Kay join us as well? Tell me truthfully.

MERLIN

I wanted you to be at ease during this journey. I knew that if we left Kay with his grandparents, away from you, your mind would be with him, always restless. I needed you to be fully with us and wholeheartedly invested in our quest. And...

NYMANNE

And?

MERLIN

Kay is not foreign to a destiny with Arthur, both brothers are fated for a future by his side.

NYMANNE

"What future? Why are my children involved in this? Yes, I was chosen by the sword, it is my mission, it is my burden to carry, I pray you spare my children these trials. Let me carry it for them!" She beats at her chest, frustratedly.

Merlin moves closer to comfort her, and embraces her tightly, as if to dissipate her fears, rocking her gently from side to side.

MERLIN

Do not worry my darling. Do not worry. This future is far ahead, when the boys will become valiant young men.

She hesitates at the word darling but chooses not to acknowledge it.

NYMANNE

I have so many questions.

MERLIN

"Ask me", he says as he continues to hold her close.

NYMANNE

When did my father have an indiscretion? How is it you even know of it?

MERLIN

Let me show you.

He continues to hold her, as they gently become suspended in mid-air, Nymanne is suddenly propelled into a trance like state. She is transported to a far-off time, and lands back in Pendragon castle, in a lone room within the highest tower. She is a witness to a younger Merlin, conversing to a more youthful version of her father.

LORD PENDRAGON

"You advised me to send my men to war! A war you assured me we would win. But at what price?" He slams his fist on the table. "My most talented general, my friend, is dead. I have lost one most dear to me! Half of my men are buried! And yet, you call this a victory?"

MERLIN

Lord Pendragon, no victory comes without sacrifice. You have sought me as your advisor, and I have done so thus far. I foretold the outcome of this war, in my mind's eye, it could not have been otherwise.

LORD PENDRAGON

I relieve you of your duties Merlin. I do not wish to see you ever again.

MERLIN

Uther.

Uther stops in his tracks. Merlin, though far younger than he, had indeed been his friend and most trusted advisor. He doesn't look back, but winces painfully.

MERLIN

Uther. Foreseeing the future is a far greater a burden than you could ever imagine. I do offer you my deepest condolences for the loss of your friend.

Nymanne is once again propelled backwards through astral travel, into a large empty hall.

LORD PENDRAGON

Elaine. I am so truly sorry for what happened. Gorlois was my dearest friend, I shall forever continue to mourn him.

He hands her Gorlois's sword and coat of armour. She sobs painfully. He embraces her in an act of comfort and support. Their embrace lasts for what seems to be an eternity. The silence settles between them.

ELAINE

"Thank you. I am better now." She attempts an awkward smile. "I am sorry to have kept you from your duties my Lord.

LORD PENDRAGON

Say no such thing. You are my responsibility now.

ELAINE

I will be fine. Do not worry.

She gently attempts to withdraw from his embrace, as she does so, they become entangled in a fervent gaze, and suddenly, he moves in and kisses her.

Nymanne is carried once more, into Lord Pendragons' chambers.

ELAINE
My love, I have come to bid you farewell.

LORD PENDRAGON
I beg of you, please do not go.

ELAINE
"What we have been living is wrong and sinful. We were drawn to one other by our common grief for Gorlois. I shall forever think of you fondly." She caresses his cheek affectionately.

She exits the room through the secret passage, but looks back longingly, one last time, before she disappears into the darkness.

Nymanne returns to the present, slightly bewildered, as though awakening from a dream. She opens her eyes to find them both suspended in an embrace. Merlin smiles deeply at her. He leans forward and kisses her gently, as they slowly float back downwards to the ground.

Scene 4

Nymanne and Merlin sit at a table in the tavern of their inn. She sits agitatedly, as the bustle of the people in the tavern helps to distract her. Merlin rests a gentle hand on her arm.

MERLIN

Be calm my darling. It will go smoothly, I promise.

NYMANNE

"My darling again. He certainly is expressive with his emotions."
She thinks to herself, startled. She wishes she could be as com-
fortable expressing her own emotions as he did. She often felt
guarded, having built so many walls during her childhood, in order to shield herself from the outside world. "We have dropped
this huge weight on the poor boy. What if he refuses to show?
What if he doesn't wish to see us?"

MERLIN

I promise you he will come. He has recognized Gawain, that was
all the proof he needed.

NYMANNE

I pray that you are right.

Very little time passes before Arthur enters the tavern, hesitant, and
yet propelled by some invisible force or morbid sense of curiosity.

ARTHUR

"Why have I come here? So that they can tell me that the man I
call father, is actually not so? Am I not betraying his memory by
agreeing to meet them?" He wonders, wrought with guilt.

Nymanne smiles broadly at her brother, she is grateful that he
has come. She feels as though she has always known him.

NYMANNE

Arthur. I am so happy you have come. I'm certain that you are filled with doubt and countless questions.

ARTHUR

Nymanne, if what you say is true then I suppose that... you are my sister.

NYMANNE

"Yes, it is strange for me as well. But I feel that I already know you, and I am so glad to have a new brother." She squeezes his arm affectionately.

ARTHUR

How am I to believe all this? If Gorlois is not my father, then who is?

Nymanne leans forward, to comfort him, and, upon doing so, touches his left arm, suddenly, images are transferred between them, as though flashing through a carousel. They both freeze, as their eyes turn upwards, flashes that last but seconds or an eternity.

Arthur bares witness to what Nymanne had seen before his arrival, through the power of Merlin's memory.

They both awaken, staring at each other incredulously. Arthur's heart beats fast. He struggles to gather his thoughts.

MERLIN

Your powers are increasing Nymanne.

NYMANNE

I...I did not intend for this to happen. I only wished to ease his pain.

MERLIN

And so, you have, I believe. Isn't that true young man?

ARTHUR

"I suppose so. Yes..." A silent tear slowly trickles down his cheek. "My father is... alive?" He looks to Nymanne for an answer.

NYMANNE

"Yes, dear brother, he is very much alive. In many ways, it seems, you have taken what's best of him." She smiles broadly, almost lovingly. "And one day soon, you two shall meet."

MERLIN

I realize that this is a most troubling turn of events for you, but I assure you that though it will be challenging at times, it shall remain positive from hereon in.

ARTHUR

What do you mean? What will be challenging?

MERLIN

My lad, your destiny is to rule this land, and I will be the one to prepare you for the difficulties that lie ahead.

ARTHUR

This is all too much; it is beyond what I can handle.

MERLIN

I understand that it is a lot to take. But your sister here has triggered a sequential turn of events. It was catalysed in Gawain's dream with a very distinct message: the time to act is now.

ARTHUR

"He will fight by my side…" He says, propelled back into the memory of his dream.

Merlin squeezes Nymanne's arm to calm her "be not afraid, all will be well". He saw that she had shrugged violently at the prospect of her son going into battle. She was not aware of what a mighty destiny awaited that young lad. How no man alive could ever compete with his valance and level of swordsmanship.

MERLIN

There is a sword that you are destined for, a sword not of this world, wielded by Wygar the elf, descended from the Vulcan God.

ARTHUR

And where is this sword?

MERLIN

"It called your sister to it. She has retrieved it, in a time of need, and it has propelled all your destinies forward. But that is a story for another day." He says, contemplating her proudly.

ARTHUR

Do you really possess such great powers Nymanne?

NYMANNE

I am learning to embrace them, dear brother. I have navigated events as they have come my way, my powers are born only to remedy them. Or perhaps I was taught to remember powers that were always within.

MERLIN

Know thyself.

NYMANNE

Socrates.

MERLIN

"You do know everything?" He smiles.

NYMANNE

Reading has been my greatest source of learning.

ARTHUR

This sword you speak of.

MERLIN

Excalibur.

ARTHUR

This sword, have you now come to entrust it to me?

NYMANNE

No, we have come to prepare you, for the time when you shall be ready.

ARTHUR

And when will I be ready?

NYMANNE

When the sword tells me that you are.

Scene 5

Nymanne wearily enters the black forest. She had left the Amazons for twelve days and twelve nights, and worried what may have befallen them during her long absence. Particularly following the battle of the guardians, the parting of the earth and the rise of the dead. She feared that all elements of life were now set on an irreversible wheel, once the gateway between this world and the netherworld had been opened.

Her suspicions were justified when she saw the hordes of women and children gathering in the camp.

NYMANNE

What is this Maeve? What has happened?

MAEVE

Ever since King Conchobar's rule, or lack of rule, chaos has ensued. There has been no security, no true law to protect the people. Men it seems have gone mad, and have taken to abusing their wives, their children, their siblings, even more so than ever before. Many women have died at the hands of their husbands. One pregnant woman was recently burnt alive by her animal of a husband, who very simply, no longer desired children. So, he set her on fire! News of our victory against the Guardians has spread far and wide through the lands, like whispers in the night. Some women have travelled great distances to seek our protection, against the men that continue to persecute them. I could not turn them away.

Nymanne looks to all the women and children with genuine concern.

NYMANNE

How will we feed them? We need to teach them to survive. Needless to say; all of this will attract unecessary attention to us. We must train these women for the battles that no doubt lie before us.

MAEVE

Yes, my Lady. I shall gather the Amazons that are fit to train.

NYMANNE

Everyone must be fit to train. A war is upon us. You understand the urgency of this, don't you Maeve?

MAEVE

Yes, I fear it is imperative. We will be perceived as a threat no doubt, and we must arm ourselves against the evils that rule this land, and the militia rule of the sleeping King.

NYMANNE

I shall try to raise a shield around the forest perimeter. In the meantime, you need to increase the vigil from above.

MAEVE

Yes. Difficult times lie ahead. But you were right to have done what you did that night, do not regret opening the gates of the otherworld. While the attack brought forth anger from the sleeping King and his religious henchmen, it has also spurred fear in their hearts. They now speak of the witch of the mist.

NYMANNE

Yes of course. A powerful woman is always considered a witch, is she not? It seems unfathomable to them that a woman should possess any powers at all. A powerful man however, is considered a benevolent wizard.

MAEVE

Speaking of which. How is Merlin?

Nymanne shifts composure, her expression hardening.

NYMANNE

Maeve, I must admit something to you. I wonder if I should.

MAEVE

What is it Nymanne? Pray tell me.

NYMANNE

I visited Merlin at his cave the other evening. He did not anticipate my arrival and seemed startled. It was as though I had interrupted a vision, or a meditation of sight into the future. And when I touched the cave walls, I had a singular vision. It was but a momentary flash.

MAEVE

What did you see?

NYMANNE

War precedes him. I saw darkness. A darkness that to him justified elements of peace.

MAEVE

What do you mean?

NYMANNE

It means that his way of thinking does not align with ours, Maeve.

War is justifiable to him. It is a necessary sacrifice. I have witnessed it before, from what he has shown me.

MAEVE

And yet this time you feel it is different?

NYMANNE

Yes. My vision was foreboding. A warning to be cautious.

MAEVE

My lady he is a powerful ally.

NYMANNE

Indeed, he is. But we must tread carefully. Do not trust him completely my friend. Though he has been all but loyal to us. Something lurks in the shadows. Let us be weary of what lies ahead. Mostly, I fear for Gawain, Merlin's visions indicate he will fight great battles at Arthur's side. We must prepare him. I wish you to train him yourself. I can only entrust this to you. He and his brother are my greatest purpose in this life.

MAEVE

If you wish that of me, then I shall do so my Lady. But... He is only a boy of twelve.

NYMANNE

"Sadly, with not another moment to lose. I fear great trials will be expected of him. He will need to arm himself against all odds." Nymanne distinguishes a faint silhouette approaching them from a distance. "Who is this young woman rushing towards us?"

MAEVE

That is Brianna, she has been waiting for days to talk to you. She
said she will speak with no one else.

Brianna runs towards her, she is a frail young girl of sixteen, with
flaming red hair, and a freckled face. Her white dress is muddied
and ripped, yet her green eyes reflect a wild determination. She
reaches Nymanne and collapses before her, weeping hysterically.

BRIANNA

My Lady, my mother has sent me here. She said you would protect us. We escaped my siblings and I from our home, but my
mother could not. I beg you, save her! He said he might kill her!
She said you of all people would understand. Please save her my
Lady, please!

NYMANNE

Who is your mother? Who will kill her?

BRIANNA

My mother is Freya, she served you in your home when you were
still married.

Nymanne is warped into a faraway memory, her demeanour
shifts and becomes shrouded in fear.

NYMANNE

Oh my God Freya! Your father has threatened to kill her? I told
her not to go back! I told her to stay with me! I told her that I
would protect all of you! Why did she ever go back, why?

Brianna sobs hysterically, her body shivering.

NYMANNE

Someone please fetch her some water.

BRIANNA

She thought he might change. He always tells her he will change. He always collapses crying and begs her not to leave him, that it's the last time he will ever hurt her. But now that he has become a member of the Kings guard, he feels emboldened by his new power. He somehow overheard that she might leave him and take us with her. He ripped a piece of her hair from her skull and sent it to my grandparents, as a token, to warn them that he alone held the power over her. Then he locked her in her room. She instructed us to run, she made us promise to leave her there, and never look back. Please save her. She said you of all people would understand.

NYMANNE

I will save her. That beast will pay for what he has done. Maeve, please take care of Freya's children in my absence.

Nymanne makes a dash towards the lake.

MAEVE

Nymanne! Wherever are you going?

NYMANNE

To fetch my sword.

MAEVE

Nymanne! You can't go alone, are you mad?

NYMANNE

Leave me Maeve! Watch the camp, everyone needs you here.

Nymanne rushes off in a blind rage. She finally reaches the water's edge and halts to call the sword to her.

Maeve swiftly catches up to her, and stands silently by her side as she contemplates the lake, sword in hand.

MAEVE

Nymanne, what did she mean by you of all people would understand?

NYMANNE

"Do not ask this of me Maeve." Nymanne winces painfully.

MAEVE

I believe I already know the answer. It helps if you can talk about it my friend.

Nymanne begins to weep uncontrollably. Maeve embraces her, caressing her hair silently by the water's edge.

Scene 6

Nymanne and Maeve stand vigil, shielded by the trees staking out the lone house before them. Four of the kings' guards stand watch at the entrance, large bearded thugs with muscles for brains.

NYMANNE

What a coward Garth is, he needed the protection of his thug friends in order to hold Freya captive. It's that wild ogre over there with the long beard, conversing with the others. There probably is another fool inside, guarding Freya, that would make five of them. Be ready for a surprise attack Maeve.

MAEVE

Wait. I have sent Horus to gather reinforcements.

NYMANNE

I told you that I am not in need of help.

Soon after Merlin and Arthur infiltrate stealthily behind them. Maeve smiles gratefully at them.

MAEVE

Merlin and your brother insisted on helping. We are worried about you, Nymanne.

MERLIN

Nymanne, you have taken this a little too close to heart, your sentiment may cloud your judgement, let us handle this, please.

NYMANNE

I have told you all that I am more than capable of doing this alone. Let us go in now please.

Arthur slips a protective hand over her shoulder.

ARTHUR

I am with you sister.

Nymanne sheds a silent tear.

ARTHUR

I did not mean to bring you sadeness, Nymanne.

NYMANNE

No, my dear brother, you make my heart so full. No sibling has ever uttered those words to me before. Maeve and Arthur, you go in to rescue Freya. Merlin and I will deal with these boars outside.

All charge simultaneously, the watchmen are caught off guard, and scramble clumsily to find their swords. Maeve and Arthur take one guard down before rapidly entering the house. Merlin and Nymanne fight the other three back-to-back. Merlin suddenly loses patience.

MERLIN

"Ic be widrife!" Merlin yells in a stunning spell, opening his arms outward at the soldiers.

An aura of white and blue light radiates outwards in circular motion and stuns the guards, as they fall lifeless to the floor, their eyes phasing to white. Garth stands alone looking round him bewildered, at his lifeless friends' bodies. Nymanne turns to Merlin inquisitively.

MERLIN

"I left this one for you." He winks.

Nymanne nods gratefully. She stands to face Garth defiantly and discards her sword to the floor. Garth stares at her and does the same, casting his sword aside. He far outweighed Nymanne in size and sheer magnitude.

NYMANNE

"Hit me. Come on hit me. It's not unusual for you after all, hitting a woman." She hisses.

Garth smiles sardonically. He charges at Nymanne like a wild beast, with his fist brandished in the air. He attempts to strike her, but she swiftly blocks his attack with her arm, and with a wild scream, she yields a full-frontal kick that radiates a bright white light, as he is propelled far backwards from the force of her rage induced magic. She charges blindly at his limp body and senselessly begins to punch his face, oblivious to the gushing blood spraying out of him with every punch.

NYMANNE

Is that all you've got, you filthy beast? Is that all you've got?

She continues to beat him, crouching over his flacid body. Maeve and Arthur exit the house with Freya and look to Nymanne incredulously. Freya rushes to her husband.

FREYA

"Nymanne stop! Please! Don't kill him! He didn't mean to!" She pleads.

Nymanne grabs his lifeless head from the back of his skull and brandishes his bloody face at her.

NYMANNE

"This is what you're protecting? THIS? This... thing? Look at what he's done to you!" She points to Freya's bruised forehead and bloodied skull. "Look at how he has treated your children! Please stop defending this animal. He shall finally get the retribution he deserves". Nymanne brandishes her sword, and stands over his lifeless body, ready to inflict the final blow.

FREYA

No! Don't kill him! I will come with you. Leave him here.

Nymanne contains her rage and looks to the beast laying passively at her feet. She knew far well, that if he were allowed to live, he would continue to haunt Freya and her children forever. She revises her strategy, grabbing his head so that he can face her, and looks into his eyes. She casts a hypnotic spell, and inhales deeply, as she expels her breath while uttering the magic words.

NYMANNE

Verto papilio... When you awaken, you shall not remember your name, your children or your wife. You shall fear all who attempt to approach you and will live out the rest of your miserable existence hidden, in a dark cave, like the vile vermin that you are.

She throws his head down in disgust, wiping her hands.

NYMANNE

Let's go.

FREYA

Nymanne, you don't understand. He promised me, he promised that this time it would be different, that he will change.

NYMANNE

Never put anything before your children's welfare. Do you hear me? They are now scarred for life by the violence they have witnessed. Look at you! Look at what you have become!

FREYA

You... You don't know what it's like.

NYMANNE

I don't know what it's like?! Has he ever told you "No one will ever love you like I do" even while he is hurting you?

FREYA

"Yes." She says, taken aback.

NYMANNE

Then don't YOU tell me, that I don't know what it's like.

118

ACT V
The Battle

Scene 1

The sleeping King sits yawning at his throne. He is startled by the sudden disruption by one of his generals, during his time of rest.

GENERAL

My King! We have received news from the villages! This witch of the mist has gained great notoriety! Whispers of her victory against the guardians has spread like wildfire. She has become a symbol of resistance for all the women! Many inspired by her actions, have stood up to their husbands and defied the guardians!

The King, in his daze, struggles to focus his attention, grasping only half of the words being uttered. He waves his hand dismissively.

KING CONCHOBAR

Women don't have the mind to gather an army! What is this nonsense you speak of? Do not trouble me with such fairy tales.

GENERAL

My King, I wish it were but nonsense. We are facing a very real revolution amongst the people. Even some of the men are beginning to question the laws of the Guardians.

KING CONCHOBAR

"The men have begun questioning? Now that is troubling indeed." He ponders "Jester what say you?"

A short buffoon dressed in colourful clothing and an elaborate hat with bells, saunters in, smiling broadly. He curtsies to the King.

JESTER

Two frogs are stuck in a well and arguing over how to escape it. One of the frogs that manages to escape turns out to be deaf, while the frog who can hear, drowns in the well.

KING CONCHOBAR

Ah yes. Wise words my Jester. Why can't you make sense like that general?

GENERAL

What frogs? What is this nonsense?

JESTER

A forest is filled with animals but suddenly there is a fire. A small bird finds a river, and desperately attempts to put out the fire by gathering water in his beak.

KING CONCHOBAR

Yes. Yes. Tell me more.

JESTER

The clouds gather in allegiance with the birds' efforts and begin to weep.

GENERAL

I am telling you we have a real insurgence on our hands, and you speak of birds and frogs!

JESTER

Hope returns because of the efforts of this one bird, let us all be hopeful birds, thank you.

The Jester bows to his fictional audience.

GENERAL

I beg you listen to me! We do not have the men to bring down this resistance! It is multiplying in numbers as we speak. We barely have enough recruits in our army to maintain your state of rule, as we continue to quash the people's advances against you.

KING CONCHOBAR

Against me? My people love me, I am their God! Am I not the sun and the moon? Does light not come directly from me? Bring in my people!

The Jester clumsily saunters out and brings in thirty men and women wearing orange sashes in honour of their King. Their eyes are empty, as they stare at their King with blind adoration.

KING CONCHOBAR

Tell me my people, do you not love me?

The orange sash people begin to speak in unison, looking mesmerised.

PEOPLE

You are our God. Mary had two born, Jesus and you. The sun comes out of you. Our blood is coloured orange, the tinge of our love for you. Glory be to you.

KING CONCHOBAR

There. You see general? My people love me.

GENERAL

"I am talking about the people rioting outside these palace walls!"

He shrieks, losing his temper and gesticulating wildly.

KING CONCHOBAR

Beware of your tongue general, or I shall have to cut it.

GENERAL

Of course. Of course. Where has my mind wandered? All is well in the best of all possible worlds. I will take leave of you now my King.

He bows and makes a swift exit.

Scene 2

ENAREES

He isn't wrong you know.

KING CONCHOBAR

"Who said that?" He says looking wildly around him to spot the intruder.

ENAREES

"I am here." He says, appearing from the shadows. "I am always here, watching you. You would do well to remember that".

KING CONCHOBAR

I have done all that you demanded of me. Why do you continue to taunt me thus?

ENAREES

Because sitting on that throne depends entirely on my good graces, I could just as easily have you removed you from it, if I so desired. You are still sitting upon that throne, because you are still somewhat useful to me. Now be a good boy and take your medicine.

He mixes a white powder in a goblet of water and hands him the concoction.

KING CONCHOBAR

I... I do not want to.

ENAREES

You will drink it, or these will be the last words you shall utter with your dying breath.

Enarees anticipates the guard's reaction.

ENAREES

Stand down you fools! My army could wipe you out in mere seconds! Do you think I ever come here alone? My men are everywhere. Some even standing amongst you." He smiles sardonically, and gestures to one of the guards, who bewildered looks to the guard standing beside him. "Now all of you. Leave us. Except for you Kissar, you shall remain here. Come, talk to me."

The guard leaves his post and comes to Enarees's side.

KISSAR

I do not mean to question you my liege, your words are descended directly from the heavens, but why have you exposed me? Now I can never resume my post and be of use to you.

ENAREES

"We have more pressing matters at hand than that unconscious fool." He gestures to the King with disgust, who begins to snore loudly.

KISSAR

This medicine you give him, is it to keep him asleep?

ENAREES

On the contrary, I give him this potion to keep him alive, can you believe it? Me helping to save a life.

KISSAR

And why should you do such a thing, my liege?

ENAREES

"Because it is easier to control a sleeping stooge of a King, and his passive blind followers, than dealing with others who consistently question our authority. That fool's life was meant to end years ago, I had envisioned it, but I needed to keep him alive and well sedated." He says, playing with a black powder.

KISSAR

What is that my liege?

ENAREES

"Kissar, I have mastered the dark magic long ago. How to control minds with my finger," He raises his long-nailed little finger, "but I have also developed a certain talent in alchemy. This is what we shall use to permanently squash the female insurgence. I am recalling you from your post, because we have a new urgent mission at hand: destroy that witch, and everything she represents.

Enarees trembles, as his neck twitches involuntarily.

ENAREES

It seems that when you consort with rats in tunnels long enough, you end up picking up their mannerisms.

KISSAR

What is so threatening about a woman my liege? Do you really believe that she is a witch?

ENAREES

Can you imagine what would happen if all the women in all the lands banded together, united? It would threaten all the monarchies of the world. Oppress women and you justify control over some, when you control some, then controlling others becomes justifiable. After women there will be social classes, if you control women, and they are subsequently considered inferior, then many things become acceptable. Why not then state that certain skin colors are beneath others as well? Control women Kissar, and everything else falls neatly into place.

Enarees throws a small portion of the powder on the floor, lights it, and it erupts in an incandescent flame.

ENAREES

I have been sent to preserve the status quo that is currently under threat, it is my life's mission. I was trained by the greatest illusionists of the world. A people that have convinced all the lands that those they oppress are the perpetrators, and that they the oppressors are the victims. They justify their murders with their need to defend their God given right. It is in fact a God given right to wield such a powerful tool of manipulation. They call it "preserving an organized chaos". We are sent to convince women that they must dress a certain way, act a certain way and serve their men. That is their god given duty. When the men are happy with this newfound power we have allocated them, they in turn accept that others may have power and control over them. When one party accepts the oppression of another, this then justifies a whole set of elaborate repressive mechanisms and subsequent abuse of rights.

That is my expertise, my delicacy, I do it with infinite delectation.

KISSAR

The pleasure of controlling others, my Lord?

ENAREES

Not only controlling others, but also convincing them that they are inferior to you, and have them take pride in blindly sacrificing their lives. It is such a thrill, to have them uphold the so-called laws of devout chastity, be the very personification of that holiness, while you make your wealth out of being the only one capable of benefitting from selling the body of others for your own pleasure. But my greatest ally in this intricate scheme of deceit, is women themselves, when they believe, when they are truly convinced by the will of God, that they are inferior, that men are destined to forever rule above them. They further inculcate that belief to their children, and then these children in turn will teach it to their children: generation upon generation of indoctrinated oppression, perfected to the very last detail. But this woman, this witch, is now threatening my life's work. She must be terminated."

He bangs his fist on the floor, as black smoke rises where his fist once was. Even whilst he admired his power, Kissar feared the darkness that reigned inside Enarees's soul. He often questioned whether they were fighting for a just cause.

ENAREES

Find this witch. Determine her weakness so that we can make an example out of her to all those women who dare attempt to defy the rule of men!

KISSAR

Yes, my liege.

He bows and exists the hall.

Scene 3

Nymanne stands outside the Dark Forest borders, the mist spell she had cast but a few days ago, begins to wane. She strikes Excalibur to the earth and chants the sacred words.

NYMANNE

Fa' fithe cuiream ort,	*A magic cloud I put on thee,*
Bho chu, bho chat,	*From dog, from cat,*
Bho bho, bho each,	*From cow, from horse,*
Bho dhuine, bho bhean,	*From man, from woman,*
Bho ghille, bho nigheau,	*From young man, from maiden,*
'S bho leanabh beag,	*And from little child,*
Gus an tig mise rithisd.	*Till I again return.*

The mist rises, fully wrapping the borders of the forest. She sighs of exhaustion, having consumed all of her energy to wield such a powerful spell. She inhales deeply, gathering her strength, and enters the forest.

She is immediately dumbfounded to see that the number of women and children in the camp has doubled. Many going about building new huts, collecting wood, whilst others still were training to fight with the Amazons.

MERLIN

My darling, why are you here? Were you not meant to watch over the children today?

NYMANNE

They are visiting their father for a while.

MERLIN

You seem concerned.

NYMANNE

Every time they are under his care, I worry about their wellbeing. He always finds reason to keep them beyond the allotted time. I often fear he will take them from me, as he has often threatened to do. It is a prevailing fear that I continue to live with.

MERLIN

I would never allow that to happen.

She turns to him and smiles gratefully.

NYMANNE

There is something you must teach me. I need to learn the power of reading and manipulating minds. I fear I shall need to use it someday soon.

MERLIN

I will teach you, if that is what you wish. But be weary Nymanne, it is a power that can cloud even your own mind, if it is used for the wrong purpose.

NYMANNE

I need only use it for one purpose, and I have only one person in mind.

MERLIN

I trust you know what you're doing. Tonight, meet me by the lake, where your powers are most connected when in proximity to the water. I shall teach you there.

Nymanne nods approvingly. She looks again at the increasing numbers gathering at the camp.

MERLIN

They have been arriving in droves. Arthur and I are doing what we can to help organize the camps, find shelter for them and teach them how to fight. Your notoriety has attracted them here, but we will not be able to host many more. I have cast a spell on the Dark Forest, should anyone enter unwelcomed, the forest will retaliate in just measure. Together with your mist spell, the forest is well protected. But for how long?

NYMANNE

I have never wished for notoriety, nor to be labeled a witch. I suppose ignorant men need to find names for something they do not comprehend.

MERLIN

I worry about your safety Nymanne. You can no longer wonder between the forest and the palace unaccompanied. The King is after you.

NYMANNE

The King and his men are fools. They would never suspect me. Particularly as I have finally agreed to create a lyrical poem in his honor.

MERLIN

You are being foolish Nymanne.

NYMANNE

I am merely keeping my enemies close, my darling. What can a halfwit figure out, if his ego is caressed with a little false praise? Let him believe that I am on his side. There is something that I must ascertain. That night when the silos caught fire. They were attempting to destroy them, in order to hide a truth. We killed a Scythian guard that night, after hearing a threatening voice in the distance. They have a powerful leader, willing to sacrifice the land in order to execute his plan. They are preparing something, endlessly plotting schemes within their tunnels.

MERLIN

There are tunnels beneath the silos?

NYMANNE

Yes, and that night, a dark demonic voice, no doubt their leader, ordered the killing of innocents, I fear the Scythians are planning to take over this Kingdom, through that puppet of a King.

MERLIN

Nymanne, we cannot endanger the lives of all those present here, at the expense of uncovering the truth. There are more pressing matters at hand. I shall investigate further, please, you must leave this matter to me.

Scene 4

Nymanne contemplates the lake. She whisps her hand caressingly to the side, as the water of the lake responds by moving in unison with her pulsating movements. She smiles, understanding that her powers were evolving, as she asserts her bond with nature.

MERLIN

It is always mesmerizing to watch you cast your spells.

Nymanne looks to her hand and shakes off the water yielding telekinesis.

NYMANNE

It is merely a playful fluctuation of water, though it brings me much joy and a greater sense of peace, I doubt it is an awe-inspiring spell. I haven't even proffered an incantation. Besides, your spells far exceed my own.

MERLIN

I surpass you only in years and experience, Nymanne. What I have learned was taught to me through decades of yielding to Druid laws, and further years of seeking solitude and a quest for truth.

NYMANNE

"By how many years do you exceed me, exactly?" She questions teasingly.

MERLIN

Do not tease me. What I am trying to tell you is, your powers are somewhat innate, you are connected to nature, to the water, and you conjure a spell based on your requirement, in a moment of need or urgency. You, Nymanne, possess a talent the rest of us have harvested and nurtured through careful learning and practice.

NYMANNE

It is true, I suppose, that nature yields to me, but it is derived from a loving exchange we have with one another. I feel a unity with nature, I trust it more than the world of men, it is an ever giving source.

MERLIN

That is the greatest power of a woman, for she is interconnected with nature. Her very cycles are regulated by the moon, her womb is the origin of life. Women ought to comprehend the full magnitude of their power.

NYMANNE

I fully agree with you. Now come, pass on some of your greatness onto me, and tutor me in the very subtle powers of the mind.

Merlin moves towards her and embraces her from behind. They both look to the calm waters of the lake, as the breeze gently soothes them. They realize, upon admiring the stars, on this very clear day, that they are witnessing the milky way in its full glory.

MERLIN

Now perhaps you are wondering, did I know of this stellar phenomenon, and did I bring you to this lake in order to seduce you? I assure you, that though I always plan and perhaps even sometimes manipulate, I am just as surprised as you are, my love.

He hugs her tightly as they are mesmerized by this wondrous sight, created by the Gods. They sit silently for many hours contemplating the pattern of the stars. He leans in to kiss her as they are both transported to a transcendental realm.

MERLIN

Now, onto serious matters. I want you to visualize the person you wish to manipulate, think of what you might tell them. Think profoundly of them, of who they are, what they are doing, and how you can access the deepest corners of their mind. Close your eyes and breathe deeply. Center your focus, your energy, entirely on that person.

Nymanne breathes deeply, as she silences her mind and connects with the divine. She enters a trance, with Merlin sitting closely behind her.

MERLIN

Can you visualize this person, in your mind's eye?

NYMANNE

Yes.

MERLIN

Then repeat after me: *Lectio animo. Dic Mihi, hva du vet.*

NYMANNE

Lectio animo. Dic Mihi, hva du vet.

Nymanne continues to inhale deeply, moving further into her trance, as she continues to chant the sacred words. She reaches a moment of total silence and void in her mind, as she communicates fully through her third eye.

Far away, in the forest of Camlann, a very shaken Mordred awakens, startled, from his slumber. He finds everyone asleep around him, as the bonfire continues to burn out quietly. He feels haunted by the waking words from his dream in that voice he knew so well: "You shall never take the children from me."

Scene 5

Nymanne approaches her father's throne in the hall of the Pendragon palace.

NYMANNE

You called for me father?

LORD PENDRAGON

Nymanne, my council informs me that you have but almost drained our stock of wheat. What have you been up to my child?

NYMANNE

Father, many battered and abused women at the hands of their spouses, have recently sought refuge with me, as well as their children. Violence is on the rise in Camlann and across the entire Kingdom, since that poor excuse for a King has come into power.

The Guardians of Morality are wreaking havoc everywhere they go, and there is no one to stop them. I have created shelters for these women and their families. Please allow me some time to teach them how to secure their own sustenance.

Lady Igraine enters the hall, having overheard her daughters' remarks.

LAY IGRAINE

Battered women? If women are being beaten, it is because they drove their husbands to beat them. It is a woman's skill to calm her husband, if she acts offensively, he will consequently beat her.

NYMANNE

Mother I beg of you. Such conversation is beneath you! Are you by any chance inferring that it is a causal situation, meaning one therefore equates to the other?

LAY IGRAINE

"Listen to my daughter, the Plato of the family." She responds mockingly.

NYMANNE

Being referred to as Plato is not an insult. How can you accuse women of being beaten as though they deserve it? You who have only known chivalry from a man. You who knows nothing of having to deal with such monsters.

LADY IGRAINE

Do you hear how she speaks to me?

LORD PENDRAGON

My daughter, you cannot speak to your mother in such a way. Apologize at once.

NYMANNE

Apologize for speaking the truth? In any case I have more pressing matters at hand. I would like to teach these women how to defend themselves. Father, I shall require several swords from the court blacksmith.

LADY IGRAINE

"Weapons for women?" She explodes in hysterical laughter. "Women are not meant to fight. They are meant to tend to their children and their husbands. A woman fighting. The very idea! I always believed I had three sons and one daughter."

NYMANNE

Yes, mother indeed. I am aware of what you think of me. I am a woman, and I can wield a sword. That is inconceivable to you. Fighting does not make me any less of a woman.

LADY IGRAINE

"That remains to be seen." She responds contemptuously.

NYMANNE

Father I will need an answer from you.

LORD PENDRAGON

Your mother is right. Women are not born to fight, my child; you would be endangering their lives by teaching them thus, Nymanne. Let me send some of my men to protect them instead.

NYMANNE

Instead of teaching them to protect themselves, you prefer them to remain at the mercy of men.

LORD PENDRAGON

My daughter, it is written in our religion that a woman...

NYMANNE

Yes, yes, let us dispense with the religious lesson I beg of you, father. I know it far too well. I take it your answer is no. I thank you for your time.

She turns to leave, in order to escape this strange world where women are born to be inferior. She did not care for such a world.

LORD PENDRAGON

What of your children my daughter? Were they not meant to be returned to you by now?

NYMANNE

Their father has yet again failed to keep his promise in keeping with the allotted time. I have been waiting anxiously to hear word. Every time they go with him, I worry that they shall never return.

LORD PENDRAGON

Be patient my child. I am certain the children will ask to be returned to you.

NYMANNE

In their last encounter, Gawain revealed his father's beliefs that boys who continue to be raised by their mother, will never grow to become real men. It is his belief that boys can only grow to become men if they undergo the hardships of loss, sporadic beatings, and learning to fight in mud and filth. Kay seemed frightened of returning to his father.

LORD PENDRAGON

I will send word to the guards to go looking for them.

NYMANNE

Thank you, father.

LADY IGRAINE

Be patient my child, do not defy him, it may lead to greater problems.

LORD PENDRAGON

Igraine. She has not defied him; he has not kept his promise. Yet again! Why must you say such things?

NYMANNE

She gives him just cause because he is a man. Men's rule above all, isn't that right mother?

Lady Igraine explodes in rehearsed sobbing.

LADY IGRAINE

How can you talk to me in this way? I only care for the welfare of your children.

NYMANNE

Yes, yes, of course mother.

Nymanne walks away exasperatedly.

Scene 6

Nymanne stands in the Great Hall of the Kings palace, in lavish dress. Her black formal gown is adorned with jewels that swish in rhythm with her nervous tremors. Her hair is coiffed, and half raised with pearls, the rest of her locks fall in waves along her back.

NYMANNE

"Why did I ever agree to this?" She berates herself for her foolishness.

MERLIN

Because we do what we must.

Nymanne looks to her right, recognizing the man's voice and turns back discretely to face forward.

NYMANNE

"What in heaven's name are you doing here?", she whispers without turning his way, "I told you I could handle this alone."

MERLIN

Our future King needs to see what he is up against.

NYMANNE

Arthur is here? Why would you endanger his life when he is not yet ready?

MERLIN

He is more ready than you think. The boy has demonstrated great talent. Besides, isn't his father of noble birth? He belongs here, just as anyone else does.

NYMANNE

To which father are you referring?

MERLIN

As far as everyone else is concerned, he is the son of Gorlois. Now breathe, and strap on that wondrous smile of yours. You shall enchant them all. I am here with you, good luck, my love.

Lady Igraine enters and walks towards her daughter hurriedly.

LADY IGRAINE

"Are you ready child? Let me fix your hair." She extends her arm and adjusts the strands of hair. Nymanne moves away impatiently.

NYMANNE

Really, there is no need mother, I am ready.

Merlin looks upon the scene, quietly amused at the sight of one who he knows to be a warrior, being coaxed by her mother like a helpless little girl.

LADY IGRAINE

"Hello. Nymanne who is this gentleman?" She asks with a broad smile.

NYMANNE

Mother, may I present to you Sir Myrdin Wylt Emrys of Wales.

MERLIN

"At your service my Lady." He kisses her hand respectfully. "Now, if you ladies will excuse me, there is a young gentleman who re-quires my attention." He winks at Nymanne and leaves.

LADY IGRAINE

Well, well, you seem to be getting a lot of attention these days. Is he a potential suitor as well?

NYMANNE

Mother, please focus. Let us enter the Great Hall.

PALACE CHAMBERLAIN

Lady Igraine Pendragon and Lady Nymanne Pendragon of Wales!

King Conchobar turns to his Jester most pleased with his triumph.

KING CONCHOBAR

Ah! She has agreed to read in honor of me, at long last. She is the only barde who has not done so, thus far.

JESTER

My King, the Lion does not need to be carried by mere whisps of words, the sun shall shine eternally on one such as you.

KING CONCHOBAR

Silence! Enough of your riddles you fool! All must write in the name of my glory. Words are carried and live forever through generations; don't you understand that? He turns to his chamberlain.

KING CONCHOBAR

Chamberlain! Bring Lady Nymanne to me. I must speak with her before she is to honor me.

The Chamberlain moves swiftly to approach Nymanne, who herself was avidly watching the movements of Arthur and Merlin from afar, before they disappeared stealthily into the crowd. She sighs nervously, wondering what they were up to.

CHAMBERLAIN

My Lady, the King requests a private audience with you. Nymanne turns to him startled and awkwardly attempts to plaster a smile on her face.

NYMANNE

Uh yes... Yes certainly.

LADY IGRAINE

My! An audience with the King. You shall be the center of attention my daughter.

NYMANNE

Mother, you are from an entirely different plane of existence.

She walks off, leaving her mother perplexed.

NYMANNE

"My King. It is an honor." She curtsies looking down at the floor, attempting to conceal her disgust.

KING CONCHOBAR

Ah my dear Lady! You have finally agreed to be part of the greats and honor your King!

She continues to look down at the floor, feeling nauseous.

NYMANNE

Indeed, my Lord.

KING CONCHOBAR

Look at her dismay at standing before her beloved King! She doesn't even deign to look upon my splendor!

NYMANNE

"How do I save myself from this torture?" She wonders desperately. "And yet what better way to muddle the waters and feign my allegiance to this fool." She thinks. "Indeed, my Lord. Your sight is far too wondrous to behold."

KING CONCHOBAR

My dear girl! I allow you to look upon our greatness.

JESTER

A woman barde. Whatever will they think of next?

NYMANNE

Ah! Do you have a problem with a woman being a barde? Perhaps I have a problem with a grown man acting like a fool.

JESTER

A woman speaks
Upon a whim,
For her thoughts like whimsical rain doth fall,

To trust a woman,
Is to trust but nothing at all.

Nymanne giggles in feigned amusement.

NYMANNE

Well done, Jester. Though you may have perhaps missed a verse in your rhyme. Pray, let me help you.

A jester jests,
And speaks half-truths,
Or perhaps no truth at all.

Where doth his allegiance rest,
If made to choose,
When his King doth fall?

The jester fumes helpless to reply. The king amused dispels the conflict.

KING CONCHOBAR

My children! There is no need to squabble. There is enough of my greatness to be marveled at by all.

Nymanne swallows hard, trying to disguise her laughter.

NYMANNE

Yes, my Lord, you are indeed, father to us all.

KING CONCHOBAR

Oh, how wonderful, "father to us all". I really do like that very much. In fact, I might very well ask my followers to refer to me as such from now on, dear lady. Jester, she certainly has run circles around you, hasn't she? Perhaps she should replace you as my barde and advisor.

JESTER

An apple is master to the tree.

KING CONCHOBAR
Here he goes again with his riddles.

NYMANNE
"Are we certain they are riddles sire?" She asks half teasingly. "Sire I really must prepare if I am to eloquently deliver your poem. Regrettably, I must now take leave of you."

KING CONCHOBAR
Very well my child.

She leaves.

CHAMBERLAIN
Sire, the Lady Ortensia of the Orange Grove, has requested an audience with you, yet again.

KING CONCHOBAR
Every time this woman comes to bask at my glory and bow at my feet, I feel a tinge of disgust. She does it with so much effusion, it is becoming rather excessive.

JESTER
I thought you cherished such moments my Lord, having others marvel at your greatness.

KING CONCHOBAR
To marvel at my greatness yes, but her spit when she sings my praise, is far too overwhelming, even for me.

CHAMBERLAIN
My Lord, Lady Ortensia of the Orange Grove.

The Lady curtsies adoringly in her orange sash, and orange dress, as she prepares to deliver her lengthy praise. In the far-left isle of the great hall, Merlin watches expectantly.

MERLIN

If it is a witch of the mist they want, then a witch of the mist they shall get.

Merlin claps his hands, and subsequently, a deafening drumming sound erupts in the great hall, as all the candles in the chandelier are extinguished plunging the hall in complete darkness. A woman's scream is heard, echoing in the silence. A blinding light then erupts, filling the room.

Lady Ortensia rises from her curtesy, her eyes blank and unblinking, as everyone stares at her with bated breath.

LADY ORTENSIA

You live in light and luxury, while you continue to plunge your people in darkness and misery. This shall mark the end of your vapid reign of evil.

She clasps her arms above her head and a mist of light spreads around her, filling the entire hall.

KING CONCHOBAR

Don't just stand there, seize that woman, she is the witch!

The guards rush to capture her, but as the mist rises, she disappears into the night.

Scene 7

The next evening, after the chaos of the ball had settled, Nymanne sneaks out of the Pendragon palace, returning to the Dark Forest. She desperately seeks out Merlin and finds him training with Arthur near a cave.

NYMANNE

Merlin, whatever have you done? You were the one to enchant that poor woman, weren't you?

MERLIN

Yes, I most certainly did. But don't feel too sorry for her. That "poor woman" as you say, is no victim, she has been consorting with the King and filling her pockets, through her alliance with him. She has mercilessly starved the people in her lands. That is why they revere that fool; they assume it is their turn to profit from the misery of others, and they do so through his protection. Do not pity such heartless souls Nymanne, ones that seek only to fill their already heavy pockets. Besides, I wanted to spare you the agony of reading your poem of false praise.

NYMANNE

But, what has become of her? Where has she disappeared to?

MERLIN

I sent her off to the farmlands that she owns. When she awakens, her serfs will finish with her, if not, no doubt the Kings guards will apprehend her.

NYMANNE

But why?

MERLIN

They now have a face to a name. I needed to protect you. You are
facing great dangers, dangers that you cannot fathom.

NYMANNE

You make light of the people you sacrifice Merlin. I wonder where
it is that you draw the line? This woman, she will either suffer
brutal murder by her serfs, or rot in jail for the rest of her days.

MERLIN

A scapegoat was needed, I did what I had to in order to protect you.

NYMANNE

But at what price?

MERLIN

A justifiable price.

NYMANNE

And who decides what sacrifice is justifiable?

MERLIN

I suppose in this very instance, when in full knowledge of the
ultimate good, that person would be me.

NYMANNE

I am of course grateful for the intention behind your actions, but
I am not certain of your argument that others can be sacrificed
for the greater good.

MERLIN

Nymanne, there are greater things to concern ourselves with, than that rotten woman!

NYMANNE

Are you referring to the Scythian leader, that man whose voice I heard that fateful night in the tunnel?

MERLIN

Not only is he a leader, but he is also a high priest! Venerated as a God by his followers. They celebrate his holiness while he clouds their minds with a mysterious white powder. He preaches religion and chastity while they capture young women and enslave them for their own pleasure! He wanted you dead. Let her suffer in your stead, she has been the cause of endless suffering herself. Justice will thus be served.

Nymanne wished she could bring herself to embrace him. But she was still troubled by what he had done. And how casually he had discarded a woman's life.

NYMANNE

Did you discover this at the ball?

ARTHUR

Yes. We also discovered a tunnel leading directly to the palace. It is actually a web of tunnels that form an underground city. It is nothing like I have ever witnessed before. Merlin and I have managed to destroy barrels of a dark powder they store as a weapon, but the Gods only know how much more of it they possess.

NYMANNE

And what is this powder?

MERLIN

It was forged by a very dark magic and possesses the power to wipe out everything in its wake. It is most certainly what erupted in the silos and destroyed the village.

NYMANNE

So, this explains why they kept the fires burning at the silos, they needed to erase the evidence.

MERLIN

Nymanne, a dark era has begun. The Scythians have taken over through the sleeping king. They do not take kindly to powerful women who challenge their state of rule. We must urgently evacuate everyone to the lands of Avalon. It is no longer safe for them here, nor for you nor your children.

NYMANNE

You are right, I must summon them at once. By this time tomorrow, their father would have returned them to me.

ARTHUR

Do what you must Nymanne. I shall gather my fellow swordsmen; they have shown allegiance to our cause and like us believe in a free world. We shall need all the help we can get.

Nymanne walks off hurriedly heading to Dosmary pool. Merlin calls to her, as she turns.

MERLIN

Nymanne, know that you are ready. Remember what I have taught you, enter his very soul, then he shall head your words. Nymanne nods determinedly and walks away.

Scene 8

Nymanne stares intently at the glistening moonlight, shimmering upon the surface of the lake. She draws energy from the moon, and crouches at the lakes edge. She removes her cloak, as her long dark hair sways with the evening breeze, the light glistens on her dark locks. With her eyes closed, she begins to channel her anger, in order to reach him.

She breathes in, fully expanding her thorax as she did so, while envisioning his face in her mind's eye. She recites the sacred words, repeating them seven times, thus inducing a trance.

NYMANNE

Lectio animo. Dic Mihi, hva du vet.

Nymanne travels as an invisible presence. She is transported to a militia camp on the outskirts of Camlann, where her children are being mercilessly trained to fight, under the rain. Every time they fall, they are yelled at to get up, push harder, to be men. She could tell Kay was very much near tears, holding them back to shield himself, feeling that his father would scold him for being weak. Her anger only intensifies at the sight of this.

She infiltrates Mordred's mind and fills it with dark memories. Memories of that fateful night. A merciless punch. A pregnant woman collapses on the floor. A child screams.

CHILD

Mommy!

A bereft man senselessly beats the door like a crazed animal. His eyes are black and absent. Mordred dragging her unconscious body up the stairs by her hair.

Mordred overcome, falls to the floor. He closes his eyes as if to block out the memories. He beats the air with his hands and covers his ears screaming.

MORDRED

Stop it. Stop!

NYMANNE

Do you remember? Do you remember Mordred? Or have you convinced yourself that these events never happened? Much like you have lied to everyone else.

MORDRED

Not me. It didn't happen. Not me

NYMANNE

Face the truth. Only then shall you be free. That black-eyed monster, that appeared in the night. If you were to look upon your reflection, what would you see?

MORDRED

I...I don't know... Stop it please!

Mordred desperately attempts to block out the voice in his mind. Pushing away the memory of that man he doesn't wish to know, the man from that night. He weaved another story. Another web of lies where she had been the culprit. Where she had abandoned him for no reason. Others were happy to believe it. Even her own family. He found great comfort in that.

Gawain rushes to his father's side as he continued to scream in agony, pressing hard on his skull to dissolve the pain of that memory. Kay stands back, calmly observant.

GAWAIN

Father! What is it? What's wrong?

Mordred attempts to push his son away; he couldn't bear the thought of being perceived as weak.

NYMANNE

Accept the truth, you must yield. Understand that it is your childhood pain that is being projected unto them. You know where they belong. Bring them back to me.

Kay stands silently under the rain. Rubbing his blistered hands that continued to ache in so many places, while his mother's voice echoed in his mind. He could hear her clearly, as though she had been standing there in front of him. Unconsciously, he understood that she was calling them to her. He knew that very soon; he would be home with her once more.

Back at Dosmary pool, the sun had risen. Nymanne opens her eyes, dismayed to face the dusk. Her heart filled with the pain of remembrance. A reality she had long buried within her mind.

She had never spoken of it. She could never admit to her moment of weakness, for allowing herself to be a victim, for not having fought back. She was a different person now. She recognized her growing strength, understanding that she would never be victim. Never again.

Scene 9

The camp in the Dark Forest was in upheaval, with everyone scrambling to gather their most prized possessions. They rushed to prepare for the promise of a new beginning, away from the misery and despair that continued to reign in this fallen Kingdom.

Maeve was instructed to make ready for evacuation, while packing only the essentials to be carried on the rafts. She had also been warned of the possibility for battle, anticipating for the likelihood of an ambush. When she saw Arthur and Merlin approaching with reinforcements, she sighed a huge sigh of relief.

ARTHUR

Maeve, these are lifelong friends that have chosen to embark on our adventure. They prefer to die fighting for our cause, rather than to serve under this nefarious King. This is Galahad, Lancelot, Percival, Bedivere, Gareth, Bors, Geraint, Gaheris, Lamorak and Palamedes. All valiant men, all ready to fight for our cause. All can manipulate a sword with mastery.

MAEVE

Welcome gentlemen, I hope circumstances will allow for a smooth transition, without the need for battle. However, I am certainly very glad to have you here with us. We leave at dawn, as instructed. The rafts will be awaiting us at the shore. Nymanne is arranging for their docking as we speak. Let us now convene with the Amazons to anticipate for potential strategies of defense, should the need for them arise.

Maeve unable to sleep that night; had a gnawing feeling that something was amiss. She rises from her tent and decides to perform last minute rounds. Everyone lay sleeping in the camp.
She checks the weapons, the rations, everything was in place. With the sinking feeling continuing to grip at her, she ventures further outwards, onto the outskirts of the camp. As she makes her way into the borders of the Dark Forest, she begins to distinguish a faint whispering, a very distant murmur. Stealthily, she approaches the clearing, where the murmur could be distinctly heard.

She finds one of the village women who had recently sought refuge with them, standing alone in a clearing. The woman is holding a glass bottle filled with a dark powder, barely perceivable through the light of the moon. Maeve carefully conceals herself behind the trunk of a tree. The woman begins to whisper certain words, words that appear to be something like a prayer, proffered in a foreign tongue. She then kisses the bottle almost lovingly and, to Maeve's horror, proceeds to light the fuse connected to it. Maeve rushes to disarm her, understanding that this was something of a weapon.

MAEVE

Stop! What are you doing? Stop!

But before Maeve could reach her, the woman manages to thrust the bottle high up in the air. It explodes in mid-flight, releasing a blinding white flare.

MAEVE

You fool! You've alerted them to our location! Who are you?
Maeve lunges angrily at her, both wield their swords.

TAURI

I am a Guardian, and you are an abomination of God! To convince
yourself that you are the equal of men, is infamy! Women must
always know their place.

MAEVE

You are a disgrace to womankind! To be in league with those
monsters, you filthy little snake!

Maeve lunges to attack, blinded by her rage, she disables Tauri's
sword, who yields helplessly on the floor.

TAURI

Don't hurt me! Please don't hurt me!

Maeve moves forward to kill her but reconsiders.

MAEVE

I shan't waste my breathe on you! Let Nymanne and Merlin have
their way with you. Now get up! Get up!

Tauri lies limply on the floor struggling to rise. As Maeve leans
forward to help her stand, Tauri swiftly extracts a dagger from
her boot and stabs Maeve deep in her chest, with a sardonic
smile lighting up her face. She leans above her.

TAURI

"Don't you know Maeve? Never trust a woman." She says, hovering above her.

Tauri takes pleasure in inflicting pain, twisting the dagger deep into Maeve's heart and looking into her opponents' eyes as she continues to writhe in agony. Maeve, gathering the last of her strength, rises to punch her. Tauri loses consciousness and collapses by her side.

MAEVE

"Get your face away from me, you snake!" She screams, pushing her away in disgust.

Nymanne, Merlin and Arthur arrive at the scene moments later, alerted by the light. They find Maeve lying almost lifeless on the floor, surrounded by a pool of her blood. Nymanne rushes to her side.

NYMANNE

Maeve! What happened?

MAEVE

They know where we are my queen, she is a spy. You must leave at once; all of you, it is no longer safe here.

NYMANNE

I'm not leaving you! Maeve stay awake for me. Besides I am not a queen, my dearest friend.

Nymanne caresses her friend's hair, holding back her tears.

NYMANNE

Can you get up? Quick Arthur, go gather everyone we must leave now! Merlin, help me carry her.

MAEVE

"No, my time is over Nymanne. Leave me here. It was an honor to have served with you. One day I know my friend, you shall be queen." She smiles, "Nostrum est futurum".

NYMANNE

Nostrum est futurum.

Maeve expels her last breath, with her eyes wide open, welcoming eternity to her. She will be with her Luana once more.

Scene 10

On the shore between Camlann and Avalon, a great battle unfolds at dawn. Merlin and Nymanne fend off the attacks of King Conchobar's army and Enarees's Militia, deploying magic disarming spells, in order to shield the women and children on the barges behind them.

Young Arthur and his knights along with the Amazon warriors, battle on the frontlines.

MERLIN

They're preparing to catapult the fire stones! Everyone retreat behind me! Arthur! Fall back!

Arthur and the Amazons swiftly retreat to board the barges and reach Merlin's side.

MERLIN

Nymanne! I need you to ward off the projectiles until I can conjure the shield.

Nymanne panick stricken, attempts to muster her strength, as she clumsily aims for a catapult being armed in the distance, anticipating the strike. It breaks at the arm in mid formation and rotates wildly, landing on a broken trunk with one end suspended in mid air, while the projectile continues to rest on the ground, with the bucket still carrying its' blazing payload.

Merlin begins to chant the sacred words of the old religion in order to raise a powerful shield. Meanwhile, Gawain, who has spotted the flaming catapult, makes a dash towards it, breaking away from the group. He jumps past them to the shore, just as Merlin manages to erect his shield. Nymanne looks to her son alarmed.

NYMANNE

Gawain! Gawain come back! Stop! What are you doing?

Gawain pays no heed to his mothers' cries and continues determinedly on his dash towards the catapult. Nymanne turns to Merlin imploringly.

NYMANNE

Merlin! Open the shield! Open it now! Gawain is out there!

MERLIN

I will expose everyone to the catapults. I can't break the shield now, are you mad?

Nymanne turns towards Merlin threatening to deploy her magic against him.

NYMANNE

Please don't make me do this. Open it now! I'm not leaving my son out there.

MERLIN

Nymanne. I beg you, think about what you're doing.

NYMANNE

I will kill you if I must. Open the shield now!

Gawain, oblivious to the turmoil he has instigated, maintains his dash towards the catapult, while fire balls like rain fall all around him. Nymanne and Merlin continue to face off in tense confrontation.

Miraculously, Gawain manages to reach the catapult unscathed by the ravages of the fire stones. He climbs to the tree branch and stands above the broken arm of the catapult, while the bucket still carried it's flaming payload. He stands, mustering all his strength whilst holding Excalibur imploringly with both hands. He bends his head down almost in prayer.

NYMANNE

"Gawain has my sword!" she exclaims, incredulous.

The blade of the sword lights up in response. Gawain takes one last deep breath and leaps onto the broken arm, fully sinking the sword into it, as it magically strikes the ground. The ball of fire is then forcefully propelled onto the army charging towards them, setting them ablaze, and causing the rest of them to retreat. Gawain then pulls the sword out, and sprints rapidly back to the barges. Merlin, confused, disables his shield to allow the boy to rejoin them.

NYMANNE

Gawain! You are injured!

Gawain's shoulder had indeed been grazed by a stray arrow. He could hardly feel the pain, his heart still pumping from the adrenaline of battle. Kay leaps to his brothers' side, and stands above him, placing his hand upon the wound, as he begins to chant the sacred words in his mind. The wound magically disappears.

NYMANNE

"Kay has healing powers?" she wonders in disbelief.

MERLIN

The army is returning, I shall attempt to disarm them with my spells. Mother Modron help us all, there is no time to raise the shield once more.

Nymanne looks desperately at everyone around her, at all those who were counting on her. She could not allow any harm to befall them. With her heart still raw from Maeve's recent passing, she begins to disconnect with everything around her, dissipating out of time, feeling only that rage building inside of her. She looks unto the water and understands that it shall yield to her.

NYMANNE

Adeochosa inna husci do chongnam frim!

Nymanne raises her arms in the air, and the water of the Cornish Sea rises upon her command; as she raises it towards the charging army, it strikes them with a debilitating force, wiping out everyone in its wake.

Merlin, Arthur and the children look to Nymanne in utter disbelief. She calls upon the mist to shield them, as they continue to sail towards Avalon. The more they approached Avalon, the more she could feel her powers rising. Before the final mist could settle, she casts one final glance at the shores of Camlann, and the recent ravages of war, with the corpses scattered upon the land. She instinctively looks upwards at the cliff of Tintagel and is startled to see her father, looking down at them, while straddling his horse.

LORD PENDRAGON

"Come back Nymanne." He whispers helplessly to the winds.

NYMANNE

"Father, it is time for you to let go." She responds to him telepathically. "One day soon, you shall meet your son", she whispers.

Pendragon bewildered, doesn't comprehend from whence the words echoing in his mind, had come. He sensed they were hers. He exhales tearfully, his lips quivering at the thought of losing her.

LORD PENDRAGON

My son?

Arthur looks up at the man in the distance, staring down from the cliff. He turns towards Nymanne and can read the pain on her face.

163

ARTHUR

Merlin, is that my father?

MERLIN

Yes.

ARTHUR

When will I meet him? When will we return?

MERLIN

When you are ready. You shall meet your father, when it is time
for you to claim your rightful throne as King. Your reign shall be
the story of legends, Arthur. Just you wait.

Slowly the mist lifts, and land is revealed, as the sun sets upon
the shores of Avalon.

End of Part 1

www.ingramcontent.com/pod-product-compliance
Lightning Source LLC
Chambersburg PA
CBHW022008120726
47992CB00001B/468